THE MYSTERY OF THE MANICHEAN MASK

THE THREE INVESTIGATORS

IN

THE MYSTERY OF THE MANICHEAN MASK

BY

ELIZABETH ARTHUR
& STEVEN BAUER

BASED ON CHARACTERS
CREATED BY ROBERT ARTHUR

Hollow Tree Press 2026

A HOLLOW TREE PRESS BOOK

Copyright © 2025
Elizabeth Arthur and Steven Bauer
Hollow Tree Press LLC

Jacket Concept Elizabeth Arthur
Jacket Design and Cover Art
© 2025 Hollow Tree Press LLC
Cover Art Pashur House

"The Three Investigators" ® & "???" ®
By Permission of Elizabeth Arthur

Published in the United States of America
All Rights Reserved

ISBN PB: 978-1-965321-36-2
ISBN HC: 978-1-965321-37-9
ISBN EB: 978-1-965321-38-6

CONTENTS

1

An Intriguing Invitation

Bob Andrews was having a bad day. At the moment, he was at work in the Rocky Beach Public Library, and although he usually liked his job, today he could hardly wait to clock out and bicycle over to the Jones Salvage Yard. There, his friends Jupiter Jones, Pete Crenshaw, and Mallory MacLeod would be finishing the move to their new Headquarters.

For years, The Three Investigators had operated out of a battered old mobile home trailer that Jupiter's uncle had given them when they'd been just starting out. But they'd outgrown the trailer, and the summer before, Jupiter had asked Mallory to come up with a plan for a new headquarters. This time around, Jupiter's aunt and uncle, Mathilda and Titus Jones, had let them convert one of the Salvage Yard's already-existing sheds. With Mallory's design, and the help of the Salvage Yard's resident carpenters Leif and Magnus Haldorsson, they'd renovated the shed that spring.

They were all very proud of their work, and with a brand-new summer stretching ahead of them, they were eager to show it off to both new and former clients. So the morning before, in his role as Records and Research for The Three Investigators, Bob had sent out an e-mail to all of the firm's past clients.

He'd attached photos of their new base of operations and suggested that if anyone had a new case for them – or even *knew* of a case – they were open and ready for business! As of now – a whole twenty-four hours later – Bob hadn't heard back from a single person he'd sent the e-mail to, which was bumming him out.

In addition, at breakfast that morning, he and his father had had an upsetting conversation. Though Bob's father made his living as a journalist for the Los Angeles *Sun*, he was also writing a book about the history of public education in the United States, and after working on the project in fits and starts for the last two years, he'd recently decided to take a day off each week to finally get it done.

This morning, after Bob's mother had left for her laboratory at Reedmore College, he and his father had been cleaning up from breakfast, and as they'd washed and dried and put stuff away, Bob had asked about his project.

His father had shaken his head a little

grimly and said he'd just had one of the chapters published in a small online magazine that dealt with contemporary culture and that not only had there been a lot of nasty remarks in the Comments section but three or four readers had written to his boss at the *Sun* demanding that he be fired.

"It's getting bad out there, Bob," his father had said. "Writers who try to tell the truth are getting as rare as hen's teeth."

"But what were you writing about?" Bob asked.

"Mostly about how black and white everyone wants to make things these days!" his father had snorted. "In a lot of schools, teachers are tossing the actual history of America out the window and making up a narrative about how people with different ethnic or racial backgrounds have supposedly always hated one another!"

"If that were true," Bob had said, "I'd never have been born."

"No kidding," said his father. "And it's not just me and your mother. The country is packed with people from different backgrounds who are happily married. It's dangerous and crazy – and just plain wrong – to act as if America is made up of a bunch of street gangs, sorted by color."

Bob had nodded, deciding not to mention that he sometimes wished his own background were a little simpler. Bob's mother's parents had escaped from Communist China during a time in Chinese history called the Cultural Revolution, and Bob's father had met her when he wrote a feature article on Chinese immigration to America. But even though that made Bob technically half-Chinese, he sure didn't feel like that. He wasn't drawn to Chinese culture, and although he loved and admired his mother, she was an evolutionary biologist and he found science a tough nut to crack.

He'd inherited his mother's genes, of course, so he looked somewhat Asian. But he hated it when people believed they understood something about him because of the way he looked. People always thought he was good at math – his worst subject – or that all he did was study, or that he'd be terrible at rock climbing.

Well, people didn't *always* think that, obviously. But when they did, they could be really stupid about it. However, the truth was that ever since he could remember, he'd been interested in the things his father was interested in –

writing and language, history and literature.

For that reason, he'd really understood why his father had been so upset at the negative reaction to the chapter he'd published online.

"But what did you say, exactly?" Bob had asked.

"The thing that seemed to really drive people crazy was when I quoted your mother – without actually quoting her, of course. I wrote that evolutionary biologists believe that racial categories are basically artificial."

"Well, aren't they?" Bob asked.

"Of course, they are!" his father had said, snorting again. "But my chapter was called 'The Manichean Mindset,' after an ancient Persian religion that believed life can be divided neatly between good and evil, light and dark – even though it obviously can't. I said it was nuts that in a lot of schools these days, kids were being taught that the world is a never-ending struggle for power between the so-called oppressors and the so-called oppressed."

All this had happened hours ago by now, but the more Bob had thought about it, the more upset he'd gotten. His father was a terrific writer, a truly hard worker, and a very good man, and it seemed outrageous to Bob that a bunch of unpleasant strangers writing to his editor about something that hadn't even been published in the Los Angeles *Sun* could actually threaten his father's livelihood – especially when everything he'd written was the truth.

Still, things had turned out better than they might have. Not only had Bob's father's editor Larry Winthrop *not* fired him, he had given him a new assignment interviewing the executive director of a local nonprofit. Their office was in Rocky Beach, but since they had public events in Los Angeles, Larry had thought there might be a lot of interest in the interview. It was scheduled for later that day, and although Bob's father had said he hadn't had much time to prepare, he was going to do his best.

By now, Bob was almost finished re-shelving books, and as he slid a battered copy of the ever-popular *Hiding In Plain Sight* into place in the horror section, he paused to look at its dust jacket. On it, the artist had depicted a malevolent figure hiding behind a painted wooden screen – a screen on which a group of children were having a picnic by a river that sparkled in the sun.

Since you really *couldn't* judge a book by its cover, whatever this particular book might be about, it was almost certainly not that, Bob thought. Then he began to push the empty cart back toward the Circulation Desk.

"My goodness, Bob. That was quick!" Miss Bennett said, looking at him over her half-glasses. "Now you'll have time to – "

"Gee, Miss Bennett," Bob said. "I'm sort of in a hurry. I've got to get to the Salvage Yard now."

"Why? Do you have a new case?" asked Miss Bennett with a gleam of interest.

"Not yet, Bob said. "But we're moving into our new Headquarters this morning."

"Well, go on then," Miss Bennett said. "You deserve it!"

Bob shrugged into his backpack, left the library, and climbed on his bike. The wind on his face felt good, and the tree-lined residential streets of Rocky Beach were always fun to ride through, when you took the time to look. The Albertsons had gotten a trampoline, and as Bob rolled by on his bicycle, their two young children were bouncing as high as they could.

Bob waved to the Albertson children, then bicycled on, still thinking about his conversation with his father, but also thinking about the fact that twenty-four hours later, he still hadn't heard from a single past client. As he biked along, the phone in his pocket buzzed. He pulled over to the sidewalk and stopped. He looked at the screen and his pulse quickened.

It was Sir Iain Anthony, the famous English actor who also directed the Rocky Beach Summer Theatre Festival. He'd been at the center of a case two summers ago, but Bob and the others hadn't heard from him in quite a while.

"Hello?" Bob said, a little breathless with excitement. "Sir Iain?"

"Bob!" Sir Iain said, in his rich, melodious stage-trained voice. "It's been far too long! How are you and Jupiter and Pete and Mallory?"

"We're fine, Sir Iain. Thanks for asking. I guess you got my e-mail about our new Headquarters!"

"Indeed I did," Sir Iain said. "It looks smashing! A very elegant place to interview clients! I'm sorry to say I don't have a case for you at the moment, but I *do* have an invitation. To the Theatre Festival's annual June Gala."

"The Gala?" Bob said. His father had written an article on the Gala for the Los Angeles *Sun* two years before. It was a yearly fund-raiser, mostly, but also an extravagant thank-you to people who had already contributed.

"I'm afraid it's short notice," Sir Iain went on, "since the Gala is tomorrow night, but when I got to the office this morning and found your e-mail, it occurred to me that there might be some interesting people at the party to whom you could give your business card. Who knows what might turn up?"

"What a great idea!" Bob said. "We'd love to come. I can't wait to tell the others."

"The thing is – and I hope this won't be a problem – this year's Gala is based on a masked Venetian ball," Sir Iain said. "You remember that scene from our production of *Romeo and Juliet* with your friend Califia? The scene where Romeo, in disguise, first sees Juliet? Those are the sorts of masks people will be wearing – masks with feathers and glitter, made to look like animals and mythological creatures. I don't suppose you have anything like that lying around?"

Bob laughed. "Not the last time I looked," he said.

"If you want to come, then maybe you could rent some masks from the Rocky Beach Costume Bank. It's downtown on Parnell Street, over the bakery. We rent their masks and costumes from time to time ourselves."

"We've got the masked part down, then," Bob said, "but what about the ball part?" He knew all too well that Jupiter disliked dancing.

"It'll mostly be eating and drinking and talking," Sir Iain said. "A bit of dancing maybe, but not a real ball. And I'm expecting a couple of people I think you know – Lyle Smith and Cornelius Patterson are coming up from Sherman Oaks, and Per Jorgensen has promised to put in an appearance. He hates these sorts of things, but I twisted his arm. I do hope you'll be able to come."

"I'm sure we will," Bob said. "In fact, we wouldn't miss it!" Bob knew that Pete would be excited to hear about Per Jorgensen – a Danish actor they'd gotten to know the same summer they got to know Sir Iain – and it would be great to see Lyle and Cornelius, who'd figured in two of their earlier cases. Lyle was a retired museum curator and Cornelius was an art restorer, so Bob guessed they must often end up getting invited to artistically-related events.

"The costume bank is run by an old friend of Charlotte Mitchell's," Sir Iain went on. "Her name is Sibyl Saskatchewan, and the last time I saw her, she seemed a bit concerned that the costume bank might be going under, so I'm sure she'll be delighted to have some new customers."

"Is Charlotte working at the Theatre Festival this summer?" Bob asked.

"Unfortunately not," Sir Iain said. "Well, unfortunately for me. But I know that she's happy living in Auburn pretty much full time now. With Connor O'Malley. She told me that The Three Investigators had something to do with that."

Bob laughed. "Not The Three Investigators. Just Pete. He's the one who got the two of them together. He turns out to be a pretty good matchmaker. He also got Charlotte's aunt Phillipa Paxton together with our friend Hector Sebastian and this summer Phillipa is staying with him in Wyoming!"

"That's a pretty good record," said Sir Iain. "Especially because I understand from Califia that Pete has also matchmaked himself with her!"

"He certainly has," Bob said. "Well, thanks again for the invitation, Sir Iain. I guess we'll see you tomorrow night."

"Brilliant! I'll look forward to it," Sir Iain said. "Ta-ta."

Bob ended the call and slipped his phone

back in his pocket. He felt better than he'd felt all day! In fact, he felt *so* much better that when he reached the Salvage Yard five minutes later, he was able to be as happy as he ought to be about how great the new headquarters looked.

The summer before, Mallory had suggested calling their old headquarters HQ1 and the new one – when it came along – HQ2. HQ2 had previously been a large but nondescript shed, covered in vertical boards that had weathered to an almost invisible gray, but now it was covered with brownish-red horizontal cedar clapboard and had a door stoop made of a block of granite that Uncle Titus had found at a quarry in Riverside County.

Even from here, Bob could see the words THE THREE INVESTIGATORS on a sign over the doorway. He loved that sign – a curved wooden board on which the words formed a curve of their own. Below the words, a chimera – made up of a golden eagle symbolizing Jupiter, a bobcat symbolizing Bob, and a bighorn sheep, symbolizing Pete – had been burned into the wood, then painted. Since Pete had had the idea for the chimera before the boys met Mallory, she wasn't part of the imagined mythological beast, but she appeared, in a subtle way, in the design of the roof.

There, the old gable roof had been replaced with a hip roof with four narrow dormers on each of the four sides and a cupola in the middle. Each of the cupola's four sides displayed a wooden sign with a single word burned into it – EARTH, AIR, FIRE and WATER, the four elements the ancient Greeks had believed were the fundamental elements of the cosmos.

To Jupiter, Bob, Pete and Mallory, they had an additional significance. Since their birthdays were in August, September, October, and November, respectively, their astrological signs included all four of the ancient Greek elements. For that reason, although the chimera might represent just the original Three Investigators, the four-sided cupola represented them all.

Everything – the renovation of the shed, the cedar clapboard, the curved sign, the hip roof, the cupola with the four elements – had been Mallory's idea, and Bob was struck again by how clever and creative she was. He'd had a major crush on her when they'd first met, but he'd eased off when he saw that she wasn't interested in him the way he was interested in her.

In fact, now, when he thought about having a girlfriend, he sometimes thought about Leif and Magnus Haldorsson's sister, Freya. The last time he'd seen her at any length had been last summer – and for short periods during the school year at the Salvage Yard. The fact that she went to Palisade Point High School and he went to Rocky Beach High meant he didn't run into her as often as he otherwise might, but he knew that Freya had had a crush on *him* even before she'd met him two years before.

To Bob's mind, it was a point in Freya's favor that she'd been drawn to him not because of how he looked but because she thought he was a good writer; she'd admired the case reports he'd posted on the Three Investigators website even before she saw his picture. He thought back to the previous summer, when Freya had introduced them to a Native American chess player named Jimmy Littlewolf, and they'd been able to help him solve a mystery about his father. Freya had actually been pretty great on that case, Bob thought.

He was just starting to walk toward HQ2 when a truck drove into the Salvage Yard. The truck was American-made – a cheerful blue – and when it came to a stop, a man climbed out of it and looked around, as if wondering where to go.

"Can I help you?" Bob asked.

He wasn't very tall – a bit under six feet, Bob thought – but he was powerfully built, with dark skin and a wide nose. He looked African to Bob, an impression enforced by the clothes he wore – a black dashiki with a brilliant-colored yoke of gold, red, and brown, and a flat-topped multi-patterned kente hat whose main color seemed to be orange. Although Bob wished the man was looking for the Three Investigators' Headquarters, he knew that wasn't very likely. The minute the man saw Bob approach, he broke into a dazzling smile. His eyes flashed with good humor. He had a wonderful face.

"This is the Jones Salvage Yard?" the man asked in a deep voice with a lilting accent.

"Yes," Bob said. "Are you looking for something in particular?"

"Not something, young man," he said. "Some one. I called yesterday and spoke to a man named Leif Hal – ?"

"You're looking for Leif Haldorsson?" Bob asked.

"Yes!" the man said, nodding. "He's holding some wood for me. I paid in advance with a credit card. Do you work here?"

"Me?" Bob said. "No. Well, yes, some-times. I mean, I help out. But I work with the Three Investigators, and we have our head-quarters here." He turned and pointed to HQ2. "So I guess I *do* work here." He turned back to the man, smiling.

"Beautiful," the man said, looking at the building. "Very fine work."

"Leif and his brother Magnus were the foremen, though my friends and I helped them," said Bob.

"Very fine, very fine," the man said.

"Would you like me to take you to Leif's workshop?" Bob asked.

"That would be good," the man said. "I thank you." That smile again. Just seeing it made Bob smile himself.

Bob led the way to the Haldorsson's workshop and then walked in. He was struck as always by how good the shop smelled – sawn wood, the fine edge of burning that came from friction, and the underlying odors of glue and linseed oil and turpentine. Sawdust danced in the shafts of sunlight streaming through the windows. Leif and Magnus were working at a table saw, and when they noticed their visitors, they turned the saw off and took off their safety goggles.

Both of them were tall and lean and very blond. Leif was the older and always cheerful and optimistic, while Magnus had a gloomy disposition, always ready to find the rip in the silver lining. Together they could sometimes seem like a comedy team.

"Hi, Bob," Leif called, coming over.

"Leif, this man says you're holding some wood for him."

"Yes!" Leif said, his eyes lighting up. He shook the man's hand warmly. "African pearwood."

"Wow!" Bob said. "Do you use that a lot?"

"I've never used it before, but a customer wanted a small table made of it, and I had some left over. It was a lucky find," Leif said.

"You do excellent work!" the man said. "This young man showed me the building you have just done."

When Leif looked confused, Bob jumped in. "He means our new Headquarters, Leif. It's so great."

From across the room Magnus said, "We're glad you're happy. Of course, if we'd had more time, we could have – "

"It's great, Magnus," Bob said. "It

couldn't be better."

Magnus smiled and nodded, accepting Bob's compliment.

"I've got to go," Bob said.

"Thank you for your help," the man said, and as Bob left, he was exclaiming over the blocks of wood that Leif had set aside for him.

"But these will be perfect!" he was saying. "This wood would make me homesick if I wasn't so happy to be in America!"

What a pity the African man *wasn't* a new client, Bob thought, as he strode back outside into the sunshine, then headed toward HQ2 to tell the others about Sir Iain's intriguing invitation. He could hardly believe how much better it made him feel to know that it might lead The Three Investigators to a new case!

2

A Meeting With Kwame Owusu

Although Mallory had heard Bob's voice through an open side-window of HQ2 and knew he'd be joining them soon, since she and Jupiter were almost finished with hanging The Three Investigators' case mementos on what they were calling the "memento wall," she wanted to keep working until he actually arrived.

By now, all but the final memento were in place. The beautiful burnished wood plaque Jimmy Littlewolf had given them the summer before – from which hung the claws of a bobcat in a chamois medicine bag, the beaded representation of the horns of a bighorn sheep, and two majestic feathers from a golden eagle – was right at the top, in the middle.

Below it was the framed CALIFORNIA, CORNUCOPIA OF THE WORLD advertisement Mallory herself had discovered and given to the Three Investigators; the damascene dagger Sir Iain Anthony had given them; the falconer's glove and gauntlet that Per Jorgensen had given them after they'd sent the so-called artist

Günther Böhm packing; the kaleidoscope Odetta Dharmapuki had given them, and all of their other mementos.

But although Mallory found each of them interesting and evocative reminders of the adventures The Three Investigators had had in the last two years, her favorite was the drawing of the Chartres Cathedral labyrinth Adam Suleiman had given them the summer before, and she'd decided to put it right in the middle of the memento wall.

As she and Jupiter together lowered the wire onto the picture hanger, Jupiter stood back and looked at the drawing.

"It was great that Adam's father helped you turn your plans for a new roof into blueprints that Leif and Magnus could work with," he said. "It saved us a lot of money. And I don't even want to think what it would have cost if we'd built a new Headquarters from scratch!"

Mallory suddenly realized that Jupiter had been making similar comments all morning.

Throughout the reconstruction of the old shed – which they'd started during spring vacation – Jupiter and Mallory had worked together really well, but although today she had sensed he wasn't quite as happy as she was about what they were up to, only now did she notice the underlying pattern of his remarks.

She supposed she hadn't *wanted* to notice, since she herself had been feeling so good about what they'd accomplished with HQ2. What *she* had accomplished, mostly, if she did say so herself. The design of the newly renovated building was really terrific.

In her plan, she'd divided the 24-foot-long by 18-foot-wide floor space into quadrants. On the left as you came in was a space to interview or entertain clients – a space with a sofa and comfortable chairs – while on the right was an informal place with lockers, a boot bin, and both beanbag and butterfly chairs – where the four of them could hang out together.

The back half of the old shed was divided into a kitchen area with a big table where they could eat and drink and do research, and an official office. On the left, there were traditional windows, on the right a set of French doors leading to their outdoor workshop, and at the back two clerestory windows set high in the wall.

It had all turned out even better than she'd dreamed it would when she had seen it in her mind's eye, and she could hardly stand the thought that Jupiter didn't entirely agree.

Still, she had to ask.

"Is something wrong, Jupiter?" she asked. "Something about money?"

Jupiter looked at her. "Not exactly."

"But earlier, you mentioned the reward we got from Matthias Mueller, as well as the honorarium we got from the Greek government for finding the Minoan Treasure."

Jupiter looked miserable. "It's just that our firm account is pretty low at the moment," he said. "When I paid the final bills for the materials, I couldn't help but see that the rewards we got from Isabella Chang and Matthias Mueller have mostly been spent."

Oh, no, thought Mallory. I was right!

Before she could say anything, the front door opened and Bob came in. The first thing out of his mouth was, "That looks great! That wall with all the mementos. Well, the whole place, really!" Mallory was glad Bob was there.

He moved at once to the area with the lockers and the boot bin where he took his bright green bike helmet and hung it on a hook, then tossed down his backpack and threw himself into a butterfly chair.

"I just met this really cool African guy,"

he said. "He was wearing a black dashiki and a flat-topped kente hat. I was hoping he'd turn out to be a client − the first client we invited into our new Headquarters! But he was just here to get some wood from Leif. Still, I actually do have some solid news!"

Looking around, he suddenly noticed that Pete was missing.

"Where's Pete?" he asked. Both Mallory and Jupiter started to answer, but in the end, it was Jupiter who actually did.

"He called earlier to say he'd been swimming at Califia's house this morning, but that he'd be leaving soon," he said glumly. "He assured me this was a one off. I hope it is." Looking mostly at Mallory, he added, "I've always known that Pete liked girls, but I thought that having *you* as what he used to call a 'girl operative' would make him happy enough so that he wouldn't also need to have an actual girlfriend."

Bob laughed at this, and so did Mallory. She herself wasn't what she'd call preternaturally attuned to such matters, but the previous summer, when a friend had invited them on a raft trip on the American River and there was an extra space, it was a pretty big clue when Pete had suggested they invite Califia.

"You *can't* be serious!" Bob said. "Anyway, Pete's as trustworthy as they come. He may be late for our meeting today, but if we ever really need him, you know he'll be there, Jupiter. I think it's great he has a girlfriend."

"It's certainly great for him," Jupiter agreed. "So what's your news?"

"It's about the e-mail I sent out yesterday – the one with the pictures of HQ2 and the announcement that we were open for business again. I was getting really depressed at not hearing from anyone about it, but on the way over here, I got a call from Iain Anthony inviting us to the Gala at the Summer Theatre Festival tomorrow night. He said we could hand out our cards and drum up some business. Lyle and Cornelius will be there. Per Jorgensen too!"

"How terrific!" Mallory said. "I'd love to see Lyle and Cornelius again." They were in their 70s and had been together for many years. Both of them were smart and funny and knowledgeable about art. Mallory, Jupiter, Pete, and Bob had been invited to a Halloween party at Lyle and Cornelius's house in Sherman Oaks the previous October, but they hadn't seen either of them since.

"What kind of Gala?" Jupiter asked – a bit suspiciously, Mallory thought.

"It's a Venetian masked ball," Bob said. "We'd have to rent masks, Sir Iain said."

"A ball?" Jupiter asked with some alarm. "Will there be dancing?"

"Not to speak of," Bob said, "and certainly not the kolo! But it's tomorrow night. We'd have to get organized and get down to the Costume Bank and rent some masks today."

Now Jupiter frowned. "How much will that cost?" he asked.

It made Mallory feel terrible that Jupiter was so focused on money – especially because she knew she was partly responsible.

After all, it had been her design that had ended up costing so much, and although, as she looked around her, she was almost bursting with pride at the end result, she knew she wouldn't be able to be happy about it, in the long run, unless Jupiter was happy, too.

"It can't be very much," she said, in what she hoped was a reassuring voice. "What would someone charge to rent a mask for a day?"

"You never know," Jupiter said.

"Sir Iain said the Costume Bank is

downtown on Parnell Street, above the bakery," Bob said. "We can ride our bikes down there as soon as Pete arrives. I hope he gets here soon now. The Costume Bank will only be open for a few more hours. Sir Iain said a woman named Sibyl Saskatchewan owns it. Maybe I should call her and reserve some masks It would be fun if she had a bobcat and a golden eagle and a bighorn sheep. We could go to the ball as our own totem animals!"

"That's a great idea," Mallory said.

"I was just looking at the chimera as I came in," Bob explained. "Though that wouldn't solve the problem of what *you* should go as, Mallory. You don't have a totem animal."

"That's O.K.," Mallory said. "You gave me my own special bike helmet and chalk last summer, and I'm on the card now, and there's no way you could change the name of the firm or the design of the chimera just for me."

"I guess not," Bob said. "But you could still have a spirit animal, couldn't you?"

Mallory felt unexpectedly flattered. Bob was always looking out for her. Pete was the one of the three who seemed most attuned to other peoples' feelings in general, but it was Bob who seemed to have a special eye out for her.

"I have no idea what my spirit animal would be," she said. "And isn't it true that you have to have a real connection with the animal?"

Bob grinned. "Do I look like I've ever met a bobcat? Pete's worked with lots of animals at the Rescue Center, but never a bighorn sheep that I know of. As for Jupiter, I don't think he's ever met an animal he liked."

Jupiter looked offended. "That's not true," he said. "I like Connor O'Malley's dog Buster. And Per Jorgensen's dog Brigitte. And I like golden eagles and bighorn sheep and bobcats, too, for that matter!"

"Anyway," Bob said to Mallory, "we sort of made our peace with it because we found out we had things in common with our totem animals. It was Pete who matched me up with a bobcat and Jupe with a golden eagle. And it was the two of us together who matched Pete up with a bighorn sheep. Maybe the three of us could come up with a good totem for you. How about a raven? Remember the carved wooden raven Jimmy Littlewolf gave you? I really liked that."

"I did, too," said Mallory. Jimmy had told her that ravens were very important in a lot of Native American cultures, and also in Scottish stories.

"A raven would be perfect," Bob said. "So should I call this woman and see if we can reserve four masks?"

Just then, however, a very familiar voice called out, "Can we come in?"

Mallory turned to see both Uncle Titus and Aunt Mathilda standing in the open doorway of the glass-paned French doors that led to the Three Investigators' outdoor workshop. The workshop had already been close to the shed, but when they'd reconstructed it, they'd moved a bit closer and tidied it up in the process. It now had a beautiful cobblestone floor – made of salvaged stone Uncle Titus himself had found for them. As he and Aunt Mathilda walked into HQ2, Aunt Mathilda put her hands on his hips and looked around.

"Well, I never!" she said. "What a transformation!"

Uncle Titus nodded, looking around him with pleasure.

"This is really something," Aunt Mathilda continued. "I knew it would be, but up until you started work, I could hardly believe that Jupiter would actually desert his old Headquarters for a new one."

"This isn't secret, the way the other one was," Uncle Titus said, "but it suits the four of you now. When I gave Jupiter that old mobile home trailer all those years ago, I never thought he'd outgrow it!"

"We still have the old Headquarters," Bob said, "and we're still going to use it from time to time. It was Mallory's idea to call it HQ1, and to call this HQ2. HQ1 seems a lot bigger since we cleared our files and mementos out of it! We also got rid of a lot of the junk and installed a swamp fan, instead of that old escape hatch we couldn't really fit through any more."

"Yes," said Jupiter. "It's a lot roomier now. We left our big computer on the desk there. We can still hang out over there whenever we want, or use it for private meetings and research."

As Bob and Jupiter talked, Aunt Mathilda had been peering here and there, and as she looked up at the new pine rafters and the open cathedral ceiling, painted white and containing the central cupola and four surrounding dormers, she murmured, "I always knew that Mallory was creative but this really beats all."

"And I like where you've put the grindstone." Uncle Titus said.

The Galilean grindstone was an engraved circular piece of sandstone that had led them to, and now served as the memento of, the first case of the previous summer — a case The Three Investigators would never have discovered if Uncle Titus hadn't brought the stone back to them from a house in the Napa Valley.

It was so heavy that the only way Mallory had been able to think to display it was to leave it outside the building, to the left of the new door stoop, on a pedestal — which was now surrounded by red geraniums and white petunias planted by Aunt Mathilda.

"Thank you both," Mallory said, feeling oddly embarrassed. "You've been so generous. We couldn't have done any of this without Leif and Magnus and all the salvaged materials you gave us — and of course, the old shed."

Aunt Mathilda swatted the air. "Don't be silly, dear. The four of you are our pride and joy."

She gave Mallory a quick hug — leaving her breathless and even more embarrassed — and then she and Uncle Titus left through the double doors. Mallory noticed that Jupiter was suddenly looking happy. When his aunt and uncle were gone, Mallory reminded Bob that he'd suggested calling Sibyl Saskatchewan.

But when Bob dialed the number, he got a recording saying that no one was available to take the call at the moment – and just then, Mallory saw through the open window that Pete was barreling between the Salvage Yard's gates. In a minute, he had joined them – still wearing his bike helmet, and with sweat streaming down his face.

"Sorry," he panted. "Just as I was leaving, Califia started telling me about a new play she's going to be in this summer at the theater. Well, not a new play, an old play called *West Side Story*. She's in the chorus, and she started telling me the plot, and I tried to make up for lost time, but – "

Jupiter looked at him.

"Anyway, it won't happen again," Pete said. "The thing is, the Theatre Festival is having a masked ball tomorrow night. Califia's been invited, and she asked me if I wanted to go. I didn't know what to say, though I sort of wanted to say yes. I mean, after all, the Theatre Festival was where I really got to know her, two years ago now. But I thought we might be starting a new case."

This long and breathless speech made Bob and Mallory laugh – and when he had finished laughing, Bob gave Pete the news that

Sir Iain Anthony had invited all of them to the Gala, anyway.

Pete still clearly felt a bit dazed from his mad dash to the Salvage Yard, but when he heard that there would be no problem with accepting Califia's invitation, he looked very pleased – and even more pleased when he heard that Per Jorgensen was going to be there, too. The Dane had been one of Pete's favorite actors even before he'd met him.

"Wow!" he said. "It'll be great to see Per again. I just read that he's going to be in something called *The Prisoner of Zenda*. He's playing two roles – the role of a king and the role of a commoner. Who else is going to be there? Is Daman Duwalia coming?"

"I don't think so," Bob said. "Sir Iain didn't mention him. But Lyle Smith and Cornelius Patterson will be there."

"They seem to like costumes," Jupiter said dryly.

"Well, so do we!" said Pete. "But Califia said that this isn't about costumes as much as it is about masks. We don't have any masks, though, do we?"

"We're going to rent some," Mallory said. "At this place called the Rocky Beach Costume Bank. It's run by a friend of Charlotte Mitchell's. We're thinking that maybe she'll have a golden eagle and a bobcat and a bighorn sheep, so the three of you can show up as your spirit animals."

"That's a great idea!" Pete said. "But what about you?"

"We thought she might go as a raven," Bob said.

"Like the one Jimmy Littlewolf gave her!" Pete said.

These guys never ceased to surprise her, Mallory thought. When she'd first met them, two summers before, they'd been a close-knit, self-contained threesome, and it had seemed almost impossible that they'd open ranks and let a stranger in.

But first Bob, then Pete had opened up to her. It had taken Jupiter the longest, but when he'd asked her, at the start of the previous summer, to design a new Headquarters for the firm, she had known that he was finally on board with having her around.

"If we're actually going to this masked ball," Jupiter said now, " – and I can see that we are – it's time to get some masks, then."

"Should I try calling again?" Bob asked.

"No," Jupiter said. "We should go."

"Let's go then!" Pete said.

Bob, Jupiter, and Mallory retrieved their bike helmets and buckled them on. As they left HQ2, closing the door behind them, Mallory smiled as she remembered how, at the end of the previous summer, the boys had given her a helmet matching theirs, and a box of chalk. Jupiter had been the one who'd decided they should be teal – her favorite color.

Since then, every time the four of them had biked together, anyone who saw them with their sleek stylized helmets in blue, green, red, and teal had known at once they were a team.

As they started to roll their bikes toward the gates, the African man Bob had mentioned emerged from the Haldorsson's workshop carrying a large block of wood. When he saw Bob and the others, he waved and smiled. They brought their bikes to a stop and waited for him to catch up with them.

"Did you get everything you needed from Leif?" Bob asked. "I'm sorry – I didn't ask your name when we met before."

"I am called Kwame Owusu," he said. "Kwame is a very common name in Ghana, but not so much in the United States. And you are called Jupiter Jones, Pete Crenshaw, Bob Andrews, and Mallory MacLeod – at least according to Leif and Magnus! I like your matching helmets. They make you look like a team!"

Since this was exactly what Mallory had been thinking, she understood why Bob had said he wished this man could be a client. He was nice, and friendly, and even though he'd come here just to buy a block of wood, he'd actually managed to memorize all of The Three Investigators' names when Leif and Magnus told him about the firm.

"We *are* a team," Pete said. "We're The Three Investigators and our Special Consultant – so if you ever need to have anything investigated, just call on us!"

Kwame Owusu smiled. "I will keep that in mind, I can assure you," he said. "Though at the moment the only thing I am investigating is how soon my wife and two children and I can become American citizens! I am glad to have met you," he added, as he turned toward his bright blue pickup truck. It was funny, Mallory thought, but some people gave off such good energy from the moment you met them that you would have been happy to sit and talk with them for hours.

Still, at the moment, they really *did* need to head out to the Costume Bank if they were to have any hope of getting the masks they wanted for the Gala, and as they pedaled off in

the direction of downtown, Mallory found herself bicycling next to Jupiter – as if by staying
close to him, she could make him feel less worried about the decision he had made to proceed
with HQ2.

3

Sibyl Saskatchewan Shares Some Suspicions

Ten minutes later, as Pete pedaled next to Bob with Mallory and Jupiter behind them, he was glad there was no problem with Califia's invitation to the Gala. He and she had been dating for over ten months now, and it was beginning to seem a bit less intense and more normal. It was nice to have a girlfriend, but also a bit strange – and it had felt even stranger since he and his friends had started working on the renovation of HQ2.

Califia wasn't as interested in either buildings or mysteries – just acting, singing, and dancing – which was fine, Pete thought. But Pete had known Bob and Jupiter for so long that when he was with them – not at school, but in the context of their cases – it sometimes felt that the three of them really *were* a sort of three-headed beast, with Califia a distraction. As they closed the distance between the Salvage Yard and Huddleson's Bakery, Pete felt the urge to talk to Bob about his morning.

"Had you heard that Califia was going to be in another play?" he asked him.

"Not until you told us," Bob said. "*West Side Story*?"

"That's right," Pete said. "Califia says it's another love story with an unhappy ending."

"Like Romeo and Juliet?"

"Califia says it's *based* on Romeo and Juliet," Pete said. "Except that it's a musical, and instead of the Montagues and Capulets, there are these two teenage street gangs – the Sharks, from Puerto Rico, and the Jets, a white gang. Califia is just going to be a member of the chorus. She's been taking voice lessons for a year now, but she says she still isn't good enough to have a major role in a musical. But she's happy to be in this one, anyway. She's getting to do a lot of dancing. Her mother is helping her out."

"That's great," Bob said. "Do the lovers die in this play, too?"

"Just one of them. The boy," Pete said. "Califia told me it ends with the two gangs getting together to carry his body off the stage. I guess, when it's over, everyone feels bad about what happened. That they hated one another for no real reason."

"That's funny," Bob said. "Just this morning my father was telling me that in a lot of schools these days teachers are teaching that people from different ethnic or racial backgrounds have supposedly always hated one another."

"If that was true, then you'd never even have been born!" said Pete.

"That's what I said!" Bob told him. "Those exact words! And Dad said that although the country's full of people from mixed backgrounds, in a lot of schools, that's being ignored and replaced with the idea of a country full of competing street gangs, sorted by color!"

"That sucks," Pete said. He pedaled for another minute. "You know, it's sort of nice to have a girlfriend. Have you thought about dating Freya Haldorsson? Everyone knows she has a crush on you."

Bob laughed. "It's funny you should say that. I was just thinking of Freya this morning."

"So go for it!"

"I'll think about it," Bob said.

Just then, they turned the corner to the street that held the bakery, and soon they were chaining their bikes to parking meters in front of Huddleson's and heading for the sign that said *Rocky Beach Costume Bank*, which had an arrow pointing upwards.

As they walked by the bakery, the smell of freshly baked bread filled the air.

"Gee," Pete said. "Maybe we should get a doughnut."

"Ixnay," said Jupiter. "Let's not get sidetracked."

The stairs to the second floor were narrow and dimly lit but they led to a spacious loft above the bakery, with high windows opening onto Parnell Street. As they walked in, a jingling bell attached to the door announced their presence, and they hadn't gotten far when a woman materialized from between the racks of costumes.

She was older, Pete thought – maybe in her sixties. Her long black hair was streaked with gray and she'd gathered it carefully on her head and fastened it with two shiny lacquered chopsticks. She was wearing a man's white button-down shirt with the sleeves rolled up and a simple red cotton skirt that reached almost to the floor. She had dark eyes, and a friendly smile. Pete could see how she and Charlotte Mitchell would be friends. They were both rather dramatic, but, perhaps because she was older, this woman seemed a bit more eccentric than Charlotte did.

"Hello, kiddos," she said. "Can I help you? Are you putting on a play? Having a party?"

"No," Bob said. "But we're going to one. Sir Iain Anthony sent us to rent some masks. He said to ask for Sibyl Saskatchewan."

"That's me!" the woman said. "Sir Iain's been keeping me busy with his Gala."

"I've never heard of Saskatchewan as a last name before," Pete said, after introducing the four of them.

The woman smiled − a little wickedly, Pete thought. "When I was much younger," she said, "not much older than you − . How old are you by the way?"

"We'll be sixteen in the fall," Pete said.

"Well," the woman said, "*somewhat* older than you, then! Anyway, I hitchhiked with my boyfriend at the time up to Canada, to an outdoor rock festival on a big lake, way up north. Reindeer Lake, in northern Saskatchewan. Lots of mosquitoes. Not that many people. We had a very psychedelic time − if you aren't too young to know what I mean by that! When we got back to California, I ditched the boyfriend and settled down near Nevada City. There were a lot of hippies up there. Everyone was changing their name, for some strange reason, so I changed mine."

That actually wasn't all that strange, Pete thought. After all, when his grandparents had come up from Mexico, they'd changed their name from Crespillo to Crenshaw.

"Still, my first name has always been Sibyl," the woman added. "It was my grandmother's name, too."

"We heard you're friends with our friend Charlotte Mitchell," Pete said.

Sibyl Saskatchewan put her hand over her heart and looked astounded and pleased.

"You know Charlotte?" she exclaimed. "Boy, do I miss her. Someone fixed her up with an artist who lives in Auburn, and she's moved in with him."

"That someone was Pete!" Bob said.

"No, really?" asked Sibyl. "Well, good work, I guess!"

"How long have you lived in Rocky Beach?" Mallory asked.

"Quite a while now," Sibyl said. "I only started the Costume Bank about ten years ago, though. Before that, I came and went a lot. I've lived all over California – up in Yreka and over near the coast in Arcata. That's where my daughter Sabrina was born. I didn't want to marry her father, so she was born out of wedlock, as they used to say." She laughed. "Wed lock. You can see why I wanted to avoid it. Anyway, it's not such a big deal now, but back then – well, I could tell you some stories. My daughter has a daughter of her own now, Scarlett."

"I see you've kept with the S names," Pete said.

"Yes," she said. "I've always been fond of alliteration."

"Us, too!" Pete said. "In fact, all of Bob's case notes use alliteration in their titles!" As Pete spoke, he gestured toward Bob.

"Bob's case notes?" Sibyl said, looking from Pete to Bob and back again. "What do you mean, his case notes? Who *are* you guys? You can't be lawyers or doctors! Not yet, anyway!"

Up to this point in the conversation, Jupiter hadn't spoken, but now he said, "We're investigators. We investigate mysteries. But we're just here at the Costume Bank to rent some masks. We're hoping you can show us some."

"I certainly can," said Sibyl. "What kind of masks do you want? I have masks that cover just your eyes – like bandit masks – and ones that cover your whole face. I've got superheroes – Black Panther, Captain America. I've got cartoon characters – Daffy Duck is popular."

"Actually," said Jupiter, "we're hoping to rent some animal masks. Do you have those, too?"

"I do," Sibyl said. "A wide variety, actually. But before I show you what I've got, I'd be interested to hear more about the four of you. Do you really investigate mysteries? What kind, exactly?"

"On our card, it says We Investigate Anything!" Pete said.

"You have a card?" asked Sibyl. "I'm impressed. Can I see it?"

"You can have one," said Jupiter, pulling out his wallet, extracting a card from it, and handing it to Sibyl. Although Pete couldn't see it, he knew that it read:

THE THREE INVESTIGATORS
"We Investigate Anything"
???

First Investigator – Jupiter Jones
Second Investigator – Pete Crenshaw
Records and Research – Bob Andrews
Special Consultant – Mallory MacLeod

At the bottom of the card was the address of the Salvage Yard, the phone number of HQ2, Bob's cell phone number, and a representation of The Three Investigators chimera.

Sibyl Saskatchewan studied the card and then looked at Jupiter shrewdly.

"I gather you're the First Investigator?" she said.

"I am," said Jupiter. "And we really *do* investigate anything. I gather from the fact that you asked to see our card that you might have a mystery for us."

"I might," said Sibyl Saskatchewan, looking at him gravely. "Though I wouldn't have mentioned it if you hadn't told me you were going to the Gala tomorrow night. As it is, I think I should tell you about it – though I should also mention that I can't pay to hire you. I'm just keeping my head above water with the Costume Bank these days."

"We don't charge for our services," Jupiter said. "Sometimes clients give us rewards, or mementos, but we never refuse to take a case just because our client can't pay. We find that solving a worthwhile mystery is its own reward."

"Pro bono," Sibyl said. "For the public good." She looked at the card again, then put it next to the cash register and took a deep breath.

"This particular mystery involves two men who run a nonprofit organization called Old Art for Young Artists," she said. "Their names are Rémy Gauthier – he's French – and Giovanni Ricci, an American, though I think his parents came over from Italy. The two of them and Gauthier's wife run the organization – and all three of them were just here!"

"Here?" said Pete. "You mean in the Costume Bank?"

"Yes," Sibyl said. "You missed them by just ten minutes. They were renting masks for the Gala tomorrow night." She grimaced and her eyes became slits. "I don't really know how much I'd have disliked Gauthier and his wife if I hadn't already known something about them, but as it was, I disliked them a *lot*!"

"Is Gauthier's wife French too?" Jupiter asked.

"No," Sibyl said. "She's Hispanic."

"What does Old Art for Young Artists do, exactly?" Pete asked.

"They give grants to young people," Sibyl said. "Their mission statement says they're dedicated to serving disadvantaged kids – between 14 and 18 – who are interested in the arts. They give money to churches and after-school programs and community groups, but they also give individual grants to young people who want to pursue some individual artistic passion."

"But that sounds great!" Pete said.

"Don't go praising them so quickly," Sibyl Saskatchewan said. "They get their money by auctioning off paintings or drawings or sculpture – or old Persian rugs or Native American baskets or Chinese pottery – that have been donated to them. But I don't think they give their grants out fairly. They say they're serving disadvantaged kids, but from what I can see, the only ones they ever give grants to are minorities."

That might not be so bad, Pete thought. Many minority kids *were* disadvantaged. Though it was true that a lot of them weren't – like him and Califia and Bob.

"How did Old Art for Young Artists come to your attention to begin with?" asked Jupiter.

Sibyl Saskatchewan looked at Jupiter keenly, then smiled.

"No flies on you," she said. "My granddaughter Scarlett wants to be a ballerina. Sabrina sends her to a pretty run-down ballet school – it's near their apartment, in a white working class neighborhood – and also, it's all she can afford. The ballet school applied for a grant from Old Art and was turned down. But another ballet school – not that far away from them – also applied for a grant and got it."

Pete could tell that the woman felt bad for her granddaughter, but so far he didn't see what the problem really was.

"But here's the thing," Sibyl went on. "The school that got the grant is more expensive and already has better teachers and equipment, and it's in a much wealthier neighborhood. But most of the kids are Hispanic, or African-American, or Asian. On their website it says that Old Art For Young Artists gives their grants on the basis of need. But from what I can see, they just give grants to minorities, regardless of whether they're disadvantaged or not."

Hmm, Pete thought. It was starting to sound a little fishy.

"Why do you think they do that?" Jupiter asked.

"I think it's all public relations," Sibyl said. "I don't think they care about the disadvantaged or the underprivileged at all. I think all they care about is looking virtuous in a really easy way so that their donations keep coming and the auction money keeps flowing."

"You think their donors will be more eager to give them art if the money is going to minorities, regardless of whether or not someone else could use the money more?" Jupiter asked.

"Yes," Sibyl said. "And it isn't just because of what happened with Scarlett's ballet school. A couple of weeks after that happened, I was talking to a woman I know who works at a big discount fabric store in downtown L.A. Old Art had just given a grant to their church. The church had applied to hire a part-time piano teacher to give free after-school lessons to kids who couldn't afford them otherwise. She said her youngest son was all excited because he loved music and wanted to learn to play the piano. This is a single mother, with four children, mind you, but the boy was turned down. She was told they were sorry but there were only a limited number of slots. And all of them were filled by minority kids. She had the feeling her son had been turned down because he was white."

"But that's not right," Pete said. "That's discrimination!"

"You bet it is," said Sibyl. "Of course,

it's a private charity, and I guess they can do what they want, but they're certainly not teaching young children anything good when they say they care about disadvantaged children but the only ones they *really* care about look a very particular way."

She paused and surveyed their faces. "Actually, now that I think about it, The Three Investigators may be the perfect people to look into this," she said. "I have a feeling that if the four of you applied separately for individual grants, two of you would get them and two of you wouldn't." She looked from Pete to Bob to Mallory to Jupiter. "If you see what I mean."

Pete did. She meant that he and Bob would be given grants just because he was Hispanic and Bob was half-Asian. He felt the beginning of one of his infamous blushes.

"That's really not the way things should be," Sibyl said, summing up. "And I really disliked Rémy Gauthier and his wife when they were here just now. Giovanni Ricci seemed a decent sort, but the other two seemed to think they were entitled to treat me like a servant.

"But what really struck me when I met these people was that if they don't care about what they *say* they care about, what else might they be hiding?"

"That's a very good question," Jupiter said. "And if these people are going to the masked ball at the Theatre Festival tomorrow night, we'll have an excellent chance to observe them without being observed ourselves."

"To spy on them, you mean?" Pete said.

"To spy on them," said Jupiter. "But if we're going to do that, we need to rent some masks."

Sibyl smiled. "And from the look of the chimera I saw at the bottom of your card, I'm betting that three of the masks are going to be a bobcat and a golden eagle and a bighorn sheep!"

"No flies on you, either," Jupiter said, smiling slightly for the first time since they'd arrived.

Sibyl Saskatchewan disappeared into the costume stacks. When she came back, she was carrying three masks, all made of leather and with large eye holes. On the golden eagle mask, the eagle's beak was dark blue — almost black — and around and above the eyes the burnished golden-brown feathers began, row upon row, getting larger, each one detailed and specific. The bobcat mask was less spectacular, but it looked very much like a bobcat — it was gray and white and tan, with tufted cupped ears, and jagged serrated sides that gave the impression of shaggy fur.

The bighorn sheep mask was dark brown – though with gold decorations of the kind Pete had seen on fancy masks for balls – and the leather horns were substantial and curled back and away from the mask's top. When Pete put the mask on, everyone hooted and applauded.

"Now, what about you, kiddo?" Sibyl asked Mallory. "What's your animal going to be? A fox, maybe? With your red hair and your Scottish accent, a fox might work for you. Foxes are smart. Associated with physical and mental dexterity. They're cunning and can see through deception. They're nimble and good in tricky situations. What do you think?"

"That sounds a lot like Mallory," Bob said, "but actually, we want her to go as a raven."

"Of course!" said Sibyl. "A raven! Ravens are very powerful. They're shape-shifters, and associated with introspection, courage, and self-knowledge, and turning problems into blessings. I made these masks, as it happens, and my raven mask is particularly good."

In very short order, she was back with a mask in which a corona of jet-black feathers surrounded two oval eyes. The beak was curved downward and the feathers curled around the head so that it wasn't just the top of the face that was covered. Somehow Sibyl Saskatchewan had etched each feather's ribs and quill; the detailing was amazing. When Mallory put it on, she looked terrific.

"So that's that, then," Sibyl Saskatchewan said, smiling approvingly.

They each took their masks and Jupiter took out his wallet.

"Now, because you're friends of Charlotte Mitchell's," the woman said, "I want to give you a discount I only give to special friends. It's 10% off, which isn't all that much. But it is something."

"Thank you," Jupiter said. Pete could tell he was pleased. He handed her the money.

"Thank *you*," Sibyl said. "I'm really thrilled that you're going to use these masks to spy on some shady characters. And since I can't afford to give you a reward, if you prove Rémy Gauthier and his wife are who I think they are, I'll not only refund the rental fee for the masks, I'll give them to you outright – for you to keep as mementos of the case!"

They thanked her, then put their masks carefully away in their backpacks. They were almost out the door when Sibyl Saskatchewan spoke again.

"Oh, I forgot to tell you. The masks are due back here by four on the afternoon the day after the Gala. Otherwise I'll have to charge you for another day. I may not be here myself, but my daughter Sabrina fills in for me, so you'll probably get to meet her."

"We'll have them back on time," Jupiter said – looking gloomy again, Pete thought. "I promise."

4

Old Art for New Artists

The next afternoon, Jupiter sat behind the old fire-scarred desk in HQ1, waiting for Mallory and Bob to get to the Salvage Yard for a pre-Gala meeting. It was good to be back, he thought. As great as the new Headquarters was, it sat right in the middle of the Salvage Yard. People walked by it all the time, and Aunt Mathilda had already made it clear that if she were looking for any of them, she'd just drop in. Here he could sit and think without fear of interruption.

The computer equipment that Zachary Hughes had given them still sat before him on the desk, but the entire feel of the old place was different – and, Jupiter had to admit, almost spacious – since they'd moved the bulk of their stuff out of it. The swamp fan Mallory had suggested they install hummed above his head, and now, instead of the sweltering summer temperatures he and Pete and Bob had learned to put up with over the years, it was cool inside – though it was still sort of dark.

He looked down at his special drawer in

the desk – the contents of which had not been altered. It still held the inked footprints he had made two summers ago when he was comparing his grown up feet with his infant feet on his birth certificate. And it still held the five counterfeit $100 bills that André Laurent had made and that Jupiter had managed to keep as a personal memento of that case – even though it was technically against the law.

He smiled ruefully at the thought that if worse came to worst, there was always that money if they totally ran out. Not really, of course. He certainly hoped some new money came their way this summer – though he could hardly see how that might happen with the latest investigation. This was one of those cases where they weren't really working for anyone in particular. Even though he'd given Sibyl Saskatchewan one of their cards, they surely couldn't be said to be working for *her*.

He hoped she'd been right when she guessed that the people who had founded and ran Old Art For Young Artists were up to something shady. Not because Jupiter wanted *anyone* to be shady, but because he was eager to get The Three Investigators' summer started – and to do *that* they needed a case. He'd just pulled up an article on the computer that suggested that the typical salary for the CEO of a nonprofit was well over $100,000.

Although he knew next to nothing about the way these so-called nonprofits worked, you didn't need to know much in order to guess that they could offer rich opportunities for fraud, deception, and embezzlement.

What was most on his mind at the moment, however, was that he was afraid he'd hurt Mallory's feelings the day before when he'd confessed to being worried about money because of how much the renovation had cost. He'd been surprised and dismayed when he'd paid the final bills and had calculated that the reward money they'd gotten from Isabella Chang would run out that summer.

Oh, well, he thought, there was nothing he could do about it now, though maybe at the upcoming meeting he should take the opportunity to discuss their income, as a firm. Pete was working at the Animal Rescue Center today – so he wouldn't be at the upcoming meeting – but since Bob and Mallory would be here any time now, Jupiter shut down the computer and headed for the outdoor workshop to wait for them there.

From where he sat, he could look through the double glass-paned doors of HQ2, which stood open to the outdoor workshop, all the way to the windows on the opposite wall. It really *was* a terrific space, he thought, and when Bob and Mallory arrived, he had no trouble starting off the conversation by saying so.

Still, very shortly afterwards, he pulled out a printout of the firm account.

"I already mentioned something about this to Mallory, but I wanted both of you to see this," he said. "I'm worried about money. To put it bluntly, if we're not very careful, we'll be broke by the end of August."

"Broke!" Bob said, studying the printout.

"Well, maybe not broke," said Jupiter. "But it would be good if we made some money this summer. Yesterday, Mallory asked me about the reward from Matthias Mueller and the honorarium from the Greek government, but though both of those were very helpful, paying Worthington, buying gas for the Flex, meals and lodging when we're away on a case – they all add up."

"And I had no idea how much windows cost," Mallory said. "If I had, I wouldn't have suggested as many as I did." She looked thoughtful. "Maybe we should each pay dues to the firm from now on. After all, we each have a part-time job, and we could all put at least half our earnings from our jobs into The Three Investigators account."

"You mean fund ourselves?" Bob said. "Through our other jobs?"

"Why not?" Mallory said. "We all love being investigators, and we could afford it."

"Maybe so," Jupiter said. "But I'd only want to consider that as a last resort. And besides, my aunt and uncle don't pay me directly – they just give me an allowance."

"Maybe we should charge our clients for our services," Bob suggested.

"There is that possibility," Jupiter said. "And some of the people we've worked for could have afforded it. But what about someone like Jimmy Littlewolf? Or Sibyl Saskatchewan? Or the cases we've taken on because we were interested in them, when we really weren't working for anyone in particular? Like the capybara smuggling. Besides, charging a fee would put pressure on us to solve the problem each time, and even though we haven't failed yet, I'd hate to feel that kind of strain."

"Anyway," Mallory said, "I like to think that what you said to Sibyl Saskatchewan is true. That solving a worthwhile mystery is its own reward. And – so far, at least – the money

The Three Investigators have gotten has been freely given, out of gratitude. Maybe that should be the model we continue to use."

"What do you mean?" Bob asked.

"Maybe we could find some supporters who like what we do and who could help us out if we ran out of money," Mallory explained. "Like the patrons of the Rocky Beach Summer Theatre Festival."

"I'd hate to go begging," Jupiter said.

"Or maybe we could set up an account at one of those online places where people support you by giving a small amount of money each month," Bob said. "That would be a lot of work, though. We'd have to offer something for their donations."

"You could just post your case reports," Mallory said. "That would give them plenty."

"I don't know about that," Bob said. "I like the idea that anyone who wants to can read what I write."

"This is actually a pretty complicated issue," Jupiter said, sounding more glum than he wanted to. "So let's not talk about it any further. I'm hoping that one of our cases this summer will be the sort that winds up making someone want to give us a reward. That would be the best outcome, I think. In the meantime, let's get to work researching Old Art for Young Artists."

"So what are we looking for?" Bob asked.

"Just basic information at this point, I think," Jupiter said. "I was very interested in what Sibyl Saskatchewan told us yesterday. She didn't put it into so many words, but she seemed to suggest that the grants this organization gives out aren't really the reason for its existence. That they're the smoke and mirrors they're using to keep people from looking too closely."

Mallory and Jupiter moved their chairs closer to Bob, who opened his laptop and typed "Old Art for New Artists" into the search bar. The website came right up. It seemed particularly flashy to Jupiter – a series of photographs dissolving one into the next, pictures of happy smiling children, a shot of three people – two men and a woman – with their arms around each other's shoulders. There were showy graphics under a banner headline and the text was studded with links to separate pages on the site.

Bob navigated to the "Who We Are" page. Sure enough, just as Sibyl Saskatchewan had said, it was a small operation.

"It's just the three of them," Bob said. "Or at least they're the only ones who have titles and salaries. This Rémy Gauthier guy is the Executive Director, and his wife Juanita is the Associate Director. Giovanni Ricci is the Chief Operating Officer."

"What does a Chief Operating Officer do?" Mallory asked.

"In this kind of an organization, I think it's just a fancy title," Jupiter said. "I bet they do everything pretty much the way we do – by agreement. I just read an article which suggests that usually a COO plans for the future and oversees what the other top brass are doing. But in this case there aren't other top brass."

Bob quickly read the paragraph under their names. "Not much to condemn them for here," Bob said. "Their salaries are really pretty low, and they say they keep their overhead to 15% of the money they raise from their auctions. All their donations are given anonymously."

"What's their overhead, according to them?" Mallory asked.

"Their salaries, and those of their employees, some offices, and a warehouse to house the donations. Incidental expenses."

Jupiter was surprised. Their salaries did

seem low. The article he'd read had said the typical salary for the CEO of a nonprofit was well over $100,000, and these salaries were under half that.

"How many employees do they have?"he asked.

"It doesn't say exactly," Bob said. He went to a page labeled "Employment Opportunities."

"Wow," he said. "This is pretty unusual. They don't have employees, *per se*. They only hire what they call 'interns,' at minimum wage, and only for three months at a time. It says the interns do administrative work and outreach — by which I think they mean finding people to donate art objects. Even the warehouse workers and forklift operators are interns."

Jupiter pinched his bottom lip. "That seems very odd to me," he said.

"What?" Bob asked. "That forklift operators only get paid minimum wage?"

"No," Jupiter said. "That they turn over their entire workforce every three months. That doesn't make sense. Just as one group of people is getting to know their jobs, they're replaced with another group."

Bob was about to navigate to another page, but Jupiter wanted to study the

"Employment Opportunities" page for a moment. At the top was a group photo of a recent bunch of interns. They were all young – late teens, early twenties. The oldest couldn't have been more than 25 or so. They were clustered together, smiling at the camera, looking like they enjoyed their work at Old Art. There were fifteen of them, and all but one were Hispanic, African-American, or Asian.

"Hmm," Jupiter said. "Do they have a list of their recent grants?"

Bob navigated to a page that listed all the grants and the amounts of the grants for the last year. Sure enough, there was a grant for a part-time piano teacher at an L.A.-area church, and a request for new barres and new mirrors from a ballet studio. There was a painting class and a writing workshop, as well as acting classes and jazz workshops and a class in video design. Some of the grants were substantial, and each was accompanied by a picture of the people who had benefited from them.

"Sibyl Saskatchewan may be right," Jupiter said. "If these pictures are worth a thousand words, Mallory and I would be foolish to apply for a grant from Old Art, no matter how badly we might need it, while you and Pete might be encouraged to do so."

Bob looked up at Jupiter. "I hope you're wrong," he said. "I don't like what that suggests."

Jupiter paused for a moment and thought. Something Bob had said before had bothered him. "Didn't you say that all the art that's donated to Old Art is done so anonymously?" he asked.

"Yes," Bob told him. "That's what it says on the Donations page."

"Don't you find that strange?" Jupiter asked. "When you go to a museum, every painting has a sign near it reading 'Gift of So-and-so.' In fact, every large donation I've ever heard of has come with someone's name attached. Buildings at colleges are named after people; even awards are named after the people who donated the money for them."

"I've seen signs at museums that read 'Gift of Anonymous,'" Bob said. "Some people don't like the spotlight."

"But aren't they the exception that proves the rule?" Jupiter said. "Most people love the spotlight. I mean, what's the ratio of So-and-sos to Anonymouses?"

Bob laughed. "About 95 to 5, I bet," he said. He pointed at his screen.

"It says here that all the So-and-sos are encouraged to have their donations appraised by a reputable appraiser – they have a list of people they recommend. That way, even if they're anonymous, they still get a hefty tax break."

"Old Art For Young Artists is tax-exempt?" Mallory asked.

Bob nodded. "The Donations page states that it's a tax-exempt organization, as defined by section – what does it say?" He looked closer at his screen. "By section 501(c)(3) of the Internal Revenue Code."

"It looks like they dotted their i's and crossed their t's," Jupiter said. "Does it say anything further on the Donations page? Since rich people expect to have their names attached, then surely Old Art has given a reason why they don't do that."

Bob read the text carefully. "Listen to this," he said, and began reading. "'We request that all donations of art be made anonymously. We welcome your gift, whether it is large or small, and believe that by keeping the process as low-key as possible we remove the unfortunate possibility that a donor would feel embarrassed or self-conscious about the size or type of contribution. Besides, the gift of helping the early career of an aspiring artist is its own reward, and we believe that the focus should be on the young people who struggle to express themselves in a culture where art is not appreciated as it ought to be'."

"Wow," Mallory said. "What a lot of hot air – especially since the donors get hefty tax breaks for giving away something they didn't want any more, anyway. What are the auctions like?"

"It just says that the Old Art auctions are held periodically, when they've amassed enough stuff to make the auction interesting," Bob said.

"Why don't you see if you can find out anything about their most recent auction?" Jupiter suggested.

Bob looked, and after a short time he opened a page and whistled. "Check this out," he said. "Talk about publicity. It's a full-page spread in the *Sun*. It looks like they turned their last auction into a major event for the society types in southern California. There were cocktails and a dinner beforehand and dancing after."

"Who paid for it?" Jupiter asked.

"Corporate donors," Bob said.

Jupiter looked down at the screen. It was

filled with photographs of handsome well-dressed people holding cocktails, dancing, sitting in a crowded room holding up numbers on the ends of little sticks.

"Do they name the successful bidders?" he asked.

"You bet," Bob said. "Here's a guy who paid $340,000 for a painting. Someone else bid $195,000 for a Chinese vase."

"This is quite interesting," Jupiter said. "When you donate a piece of art, you're asked to do so anonymously, so there's no competition. But they make the auctions as publicly competitive as possible, with tons of publicity. Then the successful purchasers take whatever they bought home and display it as evidence of their virtue."

"But that's just the way all these society types operate," Bob said. "That's nothing new."

"Maybe not," Jupiter said. "But let's see what we can find out about these two guys, Rémy Gauthier and Giovanni Ricci."

At this, Mallory opened her own laptop and got to work. Jupiter was pleased to see her and Bob working in tandem. They were a good team, and he was sure that they'd double-check and complement each other.

"Here's an article about Gauthier and Old Art," Bob said. "It says Gauthier met Giovanni Ricci about ten years ago, when they were both studying art and art history in Paris at the Pantheon-Sorbonne. They were both in the Erasmus program – a student exchange program that the European Union operates."

"Here's an article about Ricci," Mallory said.

"And here's an interview with Gauthier," Bob said.

They managed to piece together the story, which Jupiter was interested to hear. Rémy Gauthier was a French national who had met Giovanni Ricci, an American of Italian descent, when Ricci was studying in Paris as a graduate student. He'd been living in Italy, studying art, before he moved to Paris. They were both in their mid-20s when they met. Gauthier wanted a job as an art historian or curator, like The Three Investigators' friend Lyle Smith, whereas Ricci was an artist – and quite a talented one, from what Mallory was able to gather.

The two had become fast friends. After he graduated, Ricci had moved back to California and married a woman named Alyssa Millman. From a picture taken of the two of them, Jupiter saw that Millman was African-American; the caption said she was a set designer.

Gauthier had come to the United States on a one-year visa, but he'd wound up marrying an American woman named Juanita Guadalupe and had stayed in the country. The three of them had started Old Art For Young Artists five years before.

But Jupiter saw that Mallory was most interested in an article she discovered about something that had happened when Rémy Gauthier was still in Paris.

"Listen to this!" she said. "He was browsing through shops and galleries on the Left Bank and he came across a painting that he thought had been misidentified. Have either of you heard of an Italian painter named Amedeo Modigliani?"

"No," Jupiter said. Bob said he'd heard the name but really didn't know anything about him.

"Anyway," Mallory said, "Gauthier told the shop owner that he thought what he had in his shop was a real honest-to-goodness original Modigliani − one that nobody knew existed − and that the price he'd put on it was ridiculously low. He advised the shop owner to bring in an expert to look at the painting."

"Wow," Bob said. "Was he right?"

"It's unclear," Mallory said. "The shop owner was very grateful, and he called in two separate experts, but they couldn't agree. One of them said he didn't think so, but the other said it definitely was a Modigliani. The shop owner raised the price considerably, and the publicity brought in a private collector who loved the piece and bought it right away. He said he didn't care one way or the other, but he thought it was gorgeous, and he chose to believe it *was* a Modigliani.

"But the reason Gauthier got to America was because he was the guy who discovered the probable Modigliani. He was hired by this museum in L.A. as an assistant curator – which is how he got his visa."

"That's pretty impressive," Bob said. "Maybe the guy has an eye like yours, Mallory. You're usually able to tell the difference between an original and a reproduction or fake."

"Not with paintings," Mallory said. "But I'm interested in finding out more about Modigliani. It seems he was an Italian painter and sculptor, born in 1884. He studied art in Italy from the age of 14, but he caught tuberculosis when he was 18, and it later killed him. In

1906 he moved to Paris and became a serious artist — though he also became a serious alcoholic and drug addict and had no success as an artist while he was alive. He died at the age of 35, in 1920."

"He sounds like he threw his life away," Jupiter said. He knew he'd been sounding negative about a lot of things ever since he and Mallory had hung the drawing of the Chartres labyrinth on the memento wall, but even so he found the description of the artist's indulgences distasteful.

"But look at his paintings!" Mallory said. "And his sculptures!"

Mallory seemed to be wild about them, and even Jupiter found them pretty interesting. They were mostly of human figures, mostly women. Their faces were elongated, and their noses and necks impossibly stretched. Jupiter was quite sure they bore only a passing resemblance to the people who had been painted, but he had to admit that Modigliani's work was compelling, almost hypnotic. You couldn't look away.

"He was only thirty-five," Mallory said. "He died a pauper. It says he gave away his paintings in exchange for food. He left such a mess behind when he died that no one really knows how many paintings he did. Now he's among the most faked artists in the world."

"That's interesting," Jupiter said, suddenly a lot more curious than he'd been before. "So it's not that surprising to discover a Modigliani. Or a fake Modigliani. At least not as surprising as discovering another artist might be. I wonder if the painting Gauthier discovered really was an original."

"Artists have always had a hard time making a living," Bob said, "except for the lucky few that society somehow accepts. All too often their work isn't recognized until after they've died."

"That's what happened with Modigliani," Mallory said. "It says here that one of his paintings sold for over $170 million dollars a few years ago."

As Bob and Mallory went on looking at Modigliani's paintings and sculpture, Jupiter was relieved to see that, even if he *had* hurt Mallory's feelings the day before, she was clearly happy now. She was always happy when she was hot on the scent of something new, he thought. That was something the two of them had in common.

In fact, although he'd started the day feeling a bit discouraged about The Three Investigators' bottom line, at this point his discouragement had been replaced by the scent *he* was suddenly following – the thought that by tomorrow morning, The Three Investigators might be on the track of a brand-new case.

It might not be the most dynamic case they'd ever investigated, Jupiter reflected – or the one that started most fast and furiously – but after all, even a case that involved apparently boring concepts like tax exemptions and nonprofit organizations might prove to have hidden depths.

5

Many Meetings

Five hours later, Mallory sat with Pete, Bob, and Jupiter, waiting for Worthington to arrive at the Salvage Yard. She was wearing a simple cowled dress – one she'd worn to a party at Lyle Smith and Cornelius Patterson's house once – and she'd pushed her raven mask high on her forehead where it now sat like a glossy black tiara. When Mallory had put the mask on, she'd felt mysterious and powerful, almost as though she could fly.

It was funny how frequently art seemed to have to do with masks, she thought. As her mind drifted, she remembered the Janus mask she had seen a picture of the summer before when she and the others had been on the Jimmy Littlewolf case. She thought that case had been the last one on which Worthington had driven them: He'd taken them to Highland, as well as to Palisade Point, Redlands, and Pomona.

Of course, he'd also driven them up to their friend Branko Petrovic's for the rafting trip and picked them up afterwards. But he hadn't been part of that case, and although he'd also driven them to the Halloween party at Lyle and Cornelius's house, they hadn't seen him since. From the start, he'd been particularly kind to her – understanding how being an outsider with the Three Investigators could sometimes be tricky. And, of course, he was a Brit, just as she was.

Now Bob had obviously also started thinking about him. "Did I tell you that when I called Worthington to see if he could take us to the Gala, he said he'd leased a limo so that he could expand his business?"

"No!" said Pete. "Really! I'd like to see that!"

"Having a limo is good for business," Bob added. "He said we wouldn't believe the number of high school seniors he'd driven to their proms this year. He's also gotten a bunch of rich clients wanting to be more visible when they arrive somewhere fancy. I guess a limo is the modern version of a Rolls."

Mallory had seen the Rolls-Royce the day she'd first met the Three Investigators. It had had huge headlights, almost like searchlights, a lot of fancy grillwork, and big front bumpers. Years ago, Jupiter had won a contest run by the Rent-'n'-Ride Company and the prize had been the use of the Rolls-Royce, and its British driver, for thirty days.

And now, here *was* Worthington – turning into the Salvage Yard in his Mini Cooper, and then saying hello as he and the others headed toward the Ford Flex. Even before he had clambered into the back seat, Pete said, "Worthington! Bob told us you're driving a limo!"

"Indeed, Master Crenshaw!" Worthington said. "I've been driving a lot. But I've still never had clients I enjoyed as much as the three lads I used to drive in that shiny gold-plated Rolls!" He turned to Mallory, who had climbed in next to him. "And their elegant Special Consultant, of course."

"But I never rode in the Rolls," Mallory said.

"An important detail," said Worthington.

"How is the old car?" Pete asked. "I used to love it."

"I haven't seen it lately," Worthington said as he put the Flex into gear and started off. "My former employer has put it out to pasture."

"So a limousine, huh?" Pete asked. "Like one of those really long ones?"

"No," Worthington said. "A stretch limo

is as much as thirty feet long, and I generally don't go in for excess. Just a very nice sedan, with all the amenities. It keeps me busy. I've also gotten an English bulldog named Max."

"You got a bulldog?" Pete asked excitedly.

"The limo is big enough for me to take Max with me most days," Worthington said. "I just slide the window closed between the front and the back, and he settles down. My clients don't mind. And Max likes to take walks by the ocean. Now what about you? You all look a good deal older. It's amazing what a school year can accomplish. You must be almost sixteen now. Doesn't that mean you can get your learner's permits soon?"

"You bet!" Pete said. "Since we're fifteen-and-a-half, we could actually get them now, but we decided to put it off so that we can concentrate on mysteries this summer."

"We had to twist Pete's arm a bit," Bob said. "He's been wanting to drive since he was about five."

Pete laughed.

"Are you working on a case at the moment?" Worthington asked.

"Not yet," Jupiter said, "but with any luck, we will be soon. The woman who rented us our masks at the Costume Bank told us she'd also rented some to a foundation called Old Art for New Artists, and that she was suspicious of their business practices. We're going to spy on them to see what we can find out."

"Old Art For Young Artists?" asked Worthington in astonishment. "Earlier this spring I drove a couple to one of their auctions in Los Angeles. A very rich couple. I wouldn't have landed them if it weren't for the limousine! When I was waiting outside the venue, one of the other drivers suggested we go inside to see what the auction was like."

"What *was* it like?" Mallory asked.

"Very posh," Worthington said wryly. "Everyone in black tie and ball gowns. Diamonds everywhere. The auctioneer was a woman, Hispanic, and very flashy in her manner. She kept things at a steady boil. But you know, I think your contact at the Costume Bank may be onto something."

"Why do you say that?" asked Jupiter intently.

"Well, the husband of the couple I was driving bid on and bought a very expensive Persian rug. There were several other people interested in it, also, but in the end it came down to my client and another man. I've seen a lot of films about con men and cons – I've even been in a couple! – and I'd swear the other man was what you'd call a house bidder – not a buyer, but someone trying to jack the price up."

"Hmm," Jupiter said.

"Maybe I've been hanging around with the four of you for too long," Worthington said. "But I kept my eye on the man, and he did the very same thing with three other items. I mentioned it to one of the other drivers, and he said it happened all the time at these auctions – though it wasn't always the same man."

"Did you mention this to your client?" Jupiter asked.

"I didn't," Worthington answered. "I couldn't be certain what had happened, and anyway, from what I could tell, this guy could afford what he'd paid for the rug, even if someone *had* bid the price up first!"

As Worthington spoke, he was already pulling up to the approach to the Summer Theatre Festival. He drove up a long winding road to the hilltop where the renovated building that housed the Festival glowed like a jewel box in the waning light of day. The lobby was visible from the outside, and Mallory could see people milling around as they moved toward the wing where the event was being held.

"Here we are," Worthington said as he glided to a stop at the entrance. "Good luck with your spying, and have fun!"

"Thanks, Worthington," Mallory said.

"Call me a half an hour before you're ready to leave," Worthington said, "and I'll swing by and pick you up."

"We'll see you later," they all said, then together the four of them walked up the series of low, wide granite steps that led to the double glass entrance doors. The last time Mallory had been to the Theatre Festival was two summers ago, when it was putting on *Romeo and Juliet*, and Califia was starring opposite the teenage movie heartthrob Daman Duwalia. It had been a difficult case, involving a vengeful director and a mysterious dagger – but now it seemed like a long time ago.

This was especially true because that case had been the first case on which Mallory had acted independently – and successfully – in an effort to impress the boys. At the time, they hadn't yet come to understand she was eager to join their firm, and she'd been worried that if she didn't do something striking, they never would. It was great to be back after all this time. As they walked into the lobby, Mallory was immediately caught up in a whirl of color and noise. Renaissance music played softly, as an undercurrent. People stood in small groups, talking animatedly. Most wore their masks on their foreheads or carried them on the ends of small sticks, so that they could be placed over the face and then quickly taken away.

Across the room Mallory saw Califia standing with her parents and a woman Mallory had never met. Mallory thought Califia looked very pretty. She was wearing a dirndl – a ruffled apron dress that Mallory associated with Germany – with a simple black silk mask pushed onto her forehead, and as the four of them walked toward her and her parents, she waved at them with animation.

Mallory had met Califia's parents a number of times, and she always liked to see them. Califia's father was an actor who'd worked on a film with Mallory's mother just after she and Mallory had first arrived in California. Mallory knew Califia's mother less well, but she thought she was beautiful, and knew she was an excellent dancer.

As it turned out, the woman with whom she was standing – an older white woman – was a dancer, too. As Pete and Califia hugged one another a bit self-consciously, Mrs. García-

Williams said to the woman, "Pete Crenshaw is Califia's boyfriend, and these are his friends – the other Three Investigators. Guys, this is Peggy Thomas, who used to dance with Alvin Ailey. She was one of the few white members of his troupe back in the 60s and 70s, and she and her husband Clay moved out here from New York about forty years ago now, after Peggy retired."

Mallory thought that Peggy Thomas looked extremely vital for someone in her late 70s. She was shorter than Mallory and didn't weigh much more than a hundred pounds, but she was taut and slender, with decisive movements. Her white hair was cut short, and her elegant face was strong and expressive as she said hello to everyone – but when Pete said, "Where's your husband?" she suddenly looked very sad.

"He died not long ago," she said. "Califia's mother was kind enough to urge me to come with her to the Gala."

"Oh, no," said Pete. "I'm sorry. I mean, I'm sorry he died, not that I asked. Was he a dancer, too?"

"No," Peggy Thomas said. "He was a musician."

"But not just any musician," Califia's

mother said. "He was a jazz virtuoso. He played tenor sax and piano. He had a trio called the Red Hots. He got so successful that when he moved out to California, he opened his own club, The Down and Out."

Mallory couldn't think what to say to this, and neither could anyone else. While Mallory was always interested in learning new things, she had never heard of Alvin Ailey and knew nothing at all about jazz.

Still, from the conversation, and her own general knowledge, she assumed that Peggy Thomas's husband must have been African-American, like Califia's mother, and before the silence got too awkward, she managed to ask, "Did you meet your husband because he came to see you dance?"

"No," Peggy Thomas said, smiling. "The other way around. When I was dancing with Alvin Ailey, a group of us used to go to the Harlem jazz clubs. Someone we both knew introduced Clay and me, and we fell in love."

Mallory could tell from Bob's and Jupiter's silence that they were eager to get started with the investigation. Even so, she was glad she'd asked her question. Mallory knew from her own experience of losing her father that although it could be painful to talk about the person who had died, it was even more painful not to.

Still, it was time for the five of them to move on, and when Mrs. García-Williams said, "Well, see you later, Califia. Come find us if you need anything. Have a good time," they all nodded and moved off.

As soon as they were alone, Califia asked, "Have you guys been through the reception line yet?"

"The reception line?" Jupiter asked. "No. Where is it?"

Califia pointed to a line forming against the lobby wall. "It's just Sir Iain welcoming everyone, but I think we ought to go and say hello."

Califia led the way, so when the five of them got to Sir Iain, at first he seemed to see only her.

"Califia!" he said. "I'm so glad you could come. You look stunning tonight. I'm looking forward to starting rehearsals for *West Side Story*!"

"Me, too," Califia said, pointing over her shoulder to the others, standing behind her. "We're all here."

Sir Iain looked past her. "The Three Investigators!" he said." It's great to see you again! Bob must have delivered my message."

"He did," Jupiter said. "Thank you for inviting us."

"Well, I hope you'll have a good time, and that you manage to turn up something useful. See you later."

And he was on to the next guest, greeting him by name and welcoming him. It was really something, Mallory thought, to be such a fine actor and director and also to be so sociable and good with people.

As they passed beyond Sir Iain, Mallory saw Lyle Smith and Cornelius Patterson, and when Lyle turned and saw her and the others, his face lit up in a big smile and he waved madly – moving his hands as though he were bringing an airplane into a terminal walkway. He and Cornelius were standing in front of a table filled with food. A man in an immaculate white jacket stood behind it, filling cups from a large crystal punchbowl.

"Oh boy!" Pete said, making a beeline for the table. "Come on, Califia!" Califia laughed and followed him.

When everyone had caught up to Pete, Lyle gestured grandly at the table as though he'd prepared the food himself.

"Here," he said. "Take one of these little

plates and load up. The crab puffs look especially good. Make sure you get some punch."

When they had all gotten some food and were seated, Lyle clapped his hands in delight. "I'm so glad you're here," he chortled. "Iain said he'd invite you, but you never know. What a relief! Look at all these stodgy adults!"

"I don't know what to do with him," Cornelius said, shaking his head in mock dismay. "He's getting younger every year."

"Why do you call him Iain?" Pete asked Lyle. "Everyone else calls him Sir Iain."

"Yes," Lyle said, "and I would guess he's heartily sick of it. If I were him, I'd tell the Queen to take that blasted blade off my shoulder. Besides, at my age I'll be damned if I call anybody sir."

Lyle smiled wickedly and sat back in his seat. In the quiet that ensued, Mallory felt unexpectedly shy.

"Where did you get those marvelous masks?" Cornelius asked.

"We rented them," Bob said, "from the Rocky Beach Costume Bank."

"They really are fabulous," Lyle said, "like something you'd find in a costume department at one of the Hollywood studios."

"They're our totem animals," Pete said.

"The woman who runs the place made them."

"Well," Lyle said, "she's exceedingly talented." He paused. "I know it's rude to ask such questions, but aside from the fact that the Grand Factotum invited you, why did you come tonight? Surely you're not making a major contribution to the Summer Theatre Festival?"

"No," Jupiter said gloomily. "We're rather low on funds at the moment."

"Factotum?" Pete asked.

"Yes," Lyle said. "Iain Anthony himself. Isn't factotum a wonderful word? An employee who does any number of jobs. That's what Iain does around here, bless him. I called him 'grand' because of his exalted status."

"Actually," Jupiter said, "we're here because we hope we're on a case. But we really don't know yet. When we went to the Costume Bank yesterday to rent the masks, the woman who made them told us we should keep our eyes out for two men named Rémy Gauthier and Giovanni Ricci. They run a nonprofit called Old Art for New Artists."

"Hmm," Lyle said. "Isn't that interesting? Cornelius and I have been aware of those two for some time. We've been following the news about them, and to be honest, I've had my suspicions. We've met them only once, though. Charming in an unnerving sort of way."

"I thought Ricci was rather nice," Cornelius said.

"He didn't talk much, and he certainly is handsome," Lyle said. "I gather he's an American of Italian descent who married his high school sweetheart when he got back from studying art in Europe."

"Yes," Mallory said. "We saw that on the Internet. We also saw that he's supposed to be quite talented. Did you know that when Rémy Gauthier was still in Paris, he came across a canvas in a stall on the Left Bank that he thought had been painted by Modigliani?"

"What do you know about Modigliani?" Lyle asked.

"I don't know anything about him, really," Mallory said. "All I know is that I'm crazy about him. I just saw his work for the first time yesterday."

"But you loved it at once! What do you think, Cornelius?" Lyle said. "Let's adopt her!"

Cornelius laughed. "Modigliani is my favorite artist," he said. "If we could afford it, we'd fill our house with his canvases and sculptures. In fact, I'd be happy to exchange everything we own for a single Modigliani."

"Tut tut," Lyle said. "Let's not get carried away. Anyway, Cornelius's great-nephew worked for Old Art For Young Artists last summer, and he didn't like them much. He said Gauthier in particular was hot-tempered and abrupt, barking out orders and expecting complete obedience. Did you know that all their employees are interns? And that they're paid minimum wage?"

"Yes," Jupiter said. "We did know that."

"Well," Cornelius said, "since Julian is here tonight, I think I should introduce you. In September, he'll be a senior at U.C.L.A. Where is he, anyway?" he asked, looking around.

Just then, a young man with mocha skin, short corkscrew hair, a serene face, and a diamond stud in his left ear appeared, carrying a heaped-up plate of food.

"Ah, here he is," Cornelius added. "This is my great-nephew, Julian Jackson – who also likes to eat! Julian, it's a pleasure to introduce you to some young friends of ours who are investigators, and who have some questions about Old Art For Young Artists."

Mallory was impressed with Julian. He was unusually tall – well over six feet – and he also had unusual self-confidence. When Lyle urged him to tell The Three Investigators everything he knew about Old Art, Julian said he'd gotten the internship not because he was majoring in Renaissance Art in college – although he was – but because he threw pots as a hobby.

"That's the way it was with most of the interns I worked with," he said. "Last summer, there was a printmaker, a woman who made silver jewelry, a guy who did stained glass, a jazz pianist, and a dancer. Of all the people they hired, only one or two were really serious about actually doing art, and I was the only one who was studying it. Not that they knew I was studying it when they hired me. They didn't ask questions about people's education, or even their job experience, on their application."

"Do you know anyone working at Old Art now?" Jupiter asked.

"Actually, I do," Julian responded. "One of my friends from college applied to work there this summer. I tried to talk him out of it, but he didn't listen to me. He's also studying Art History – but in his case, it's the history of the avant-garde in Paris in the early twentieth century. His hobby is putting pieces of seaweed on pieces of paper, letting them dry, then selling them as note cards!"

"Would you be willing to introduce us if our inquiries turn into something?" Jupiter asked.

"Absolutely," Julian said. "His name is Randy Foreman, and I'm going to be seeing him the day after tomorrow. We'll both be selling our stuff at Palisade Point Farmer's Market. Why don't you give me a cell phone number, and after I've seen him, I can call you?"

"That would be great," said Jupiter, looking around for Bob – but since Bob was talking to Lyle and Cornelius just then, Mallory gave her own cell phone number to Julian.

"Thanks," Julian said. "I'll call you on Sunday sometime."

"Terrific," Mallory said. "In the meantime, if you've seen Giovanni Ricci and Rémy Gauthier since you got here, can you point them out to us?"

Julian scanned the room, then pointed at two men and a woman who were standing and talking not twenty feet away. Wow, Mallory thought. Although she'd seen pictures online, it was always different when you saw people in person – and the thing that really struck her as she saw these particular three people was that, while both of the men were handsome, in different ways, Juanita Guadalupe was supremely ordinary-looking.

She had short black wavy hair, a round face, bright red lips, and a space between her front teeth. She was pleasant enough, and Mallory could imagine that at an auction she might seem flashy, but her husband, Rémy Gauthier, was a Frenchman with classic Gallic good looks – and from what she could see, he knew it.

To be blunt about it, Mallory thought, a loving marriage between an extremely attractive man and a far less attractive woman was a rarity in nature, and in this particular case, nothing she was seeing so far suggested that Rémy and Juanita could be anything but business partners.

As for Giovanni Ricci, he was also, as Lyle had mentioned, quite handsome, but his smile was winning and his body language open and welcoming. To Mallory, he didn't look particularly Italian, but he *did* look like someone who might be genuinely interested in art.

As Mallory watched, all three of them lowered their masks from their foreheads to their faces and started walking away into the crowd.

"Now that we know who they are," Jupiter said, "we should put our masks on before they see us, and keep them on. When we eavesdrop, we want to keep track of everything they say to one another, or to anyone else. It's important they don't know who we are. If this turns into a real case, we don't want to be recognized as anyone they've seen or met here tonight. We want to be as anonymous without our masks on as we will be tonight, with them."

"You've changed your mind about handing out our card, then?" Bob asked.

"Yes," Jupiter said. "Not a good idea. Let's concentrate on Gauthier and Ricci. And if we're here undercover, we can hardly give out our card to people we don't know."

"How do you want to do this?" Bob asked.

"In shifts, I think," Jupiter said. "A whole bunch of us hanging around at once would look pretty suspicious. Bob, why don't you and Mallory take the first shift, and then after a while, Pete and Califia and I will take over."

"That's a plan," Bob said.

"Seeing the four of you in action is quite inspiring," Lyle said. "Good luck."

They had thanked Julian Jackson, said goodbye to Lyle and Cornelius, and started off in the direction of Rémy Gauthier and Giovanni Ricci when Pete suddenly said, "Look! It's Per Jorgensen! And I bet that's the woman we met last summer – the camera woman, Jo March!"

Since Per hadn't made any particular effort to dress up – though he *was* wearing a simple wolf mask, and so was his female companion – Mallory was fairly certain that Pete was right.

"Come on!" Pete said, as he led the way. But just then, Mallory saw that Rémy Gauthier, Juanita Guadalupe, and Giovanni Ricci were drifting toward a distant corner of the room. Bob had been watching their movements, too.

He nodded to Mallory, then said to the others, "Say hello to Per for us. Mallory and I have got to go." He lowered his mask, and Mallory did the same. She had liked Jo March the one time she'd met her, and she was glad to think she and Per were dating, but although in a way she was sorry she couldn't go to say hello to the two of them, in another way she was relieved. While she was better at managing her anxiety at big gatherings than she'd been when she was younger, she still found meeting so many people so quickly a little daunting.

She thought back to what Sibyl Saskatchewan had said about ravens being shapeshifters and wondered if being a raven for the evening would give her a special edge. Probably not, she thought. She just hoped that she and Bob could get close enough to their targets to hear the sort of things that ravens supposedly sometimes heard – or said – in Scottish folk tales. After all, it was well past time to discover if The Three Investigators had actually found their first case of the summer!

6

An Eavesdropping Triumph

As Bob and Mallory followed Rémy Gauthier, Juanita Guadalupe, and Giovanni Ricci across the packed room, Bob was glad to be wearing the bobcat mask. It made him feel stealthy and cunning, capable of stalking prey, and that was good, he thought. Although pretending not to be listening to someone while you really *were* might not be the most challenging acting job anyone had ever done, it was still acting, and Bob was a terrible actor.

His father said this was because he was such an honest person, but the truth was, Bob lacked a sometimes very useful talent for pretending. When he tried to pretend to be anyone other than himself, he gave himself away in no time with what the others called his deer-in-the-headlights look.

Wearing a mask provided cover, and as he moved through the crowd, anonymous, unencumbered by social obligations or other peoples' expectations, he found he liked the fact that no one could make assumptions about who he was. Given the way the mask covered his face, he didn't think that anyone who saw him would even guess that he was half-Asian.

He was strangely glad of that, maybe because, as he and Mallory followed the trio that had founded Old Art For Young Artists, he found himself thinking about the conversation The Three Investigators had had with Sibyl Saskatchewan.

Ever since she'd suggested that if the four of them applied for a grant from the organization, he and Pete would stand a good chance while Mallory and Jupiter wouldn't, Bob had been trying to disbelieve her – though without success.

Bob just couldn't shake it off, somehow. It seemed so horrible to think that anyone would judge the four of them in such a superficial way, and not as the individuals they were – each of them unique, and uniquely suited to working together as a group. If Old Art For Young Artists *was* up to something illegal – or even just immoral – he hoped they could nail them. He didn't want to live in a world where people were judged not by who they were but solely by what they looked like – or who their ancestors had been.

Bob's parents were very different from each other, but they'd both raised him to believe that everyone had the same basic human rights and should have equal opportunities, and that if someone was rewarded, it should be because they deserved it and had earned it, and if they were helped, it should be because they needed it. But the people they were following at the Gala seemed to believe something else entirely.

"Where do you think they're heading?" he said to Mallory.

"I'm not sure they're headed anywhere in particular," Mallory said. "I think they're just circulating. Glad-handing."

Sure enough, they seemed to be working the room, pausing to shake hands and chat for a minute, before moving on. As the three of them wove among the masked and sometimes costumed crowd, Bob couldn't figure out how the trio knew who it was they were stopping to talk to. Everyone was a stranger to him – and at the moment, he felt like a bit disoriented.

Even with the mask on, he was glad Mallory was with him. She was an excellent actor and had proven it several times over the last two summers. She was a quick thinker, able to come up with excuses and explanations at the drop of a hat, and an excellent improviser, whereas if things changed too quickly in a tense situation, Bob got utterly tongue-tied.

Bob was keeping his eyes on their target when he accidentally bumped into an older man. He apologized profusely, and when he turned back, for a moment he couldn't find the trio. He felt a rising tide of panic until he realized Mallory hadn't lost track of them.

He caught up to her. "I thought I'd lost them for a minute," he said.

"They're right over there," she replied. "Let's get our skates on."

Bob followed Mallory's finger and saw that the three were now talking to a plump and well-dressed couple in their sixties – both of whom held their masks on the ends of short sticks. Because of where they were standing, Bob and Mallory were finally able to sidle close. They pretended to be engrossed in their own conversation, but both of them strained to hear what was being said.

At first it was just small talk. Rémy Gauthier was complimenting the woman on her mask, which, Bob saw, was really nothing special. Gauthier seemed to be playing up his own French accent, as though it were the height of sophistication, while Juanita Guadalupe said how grateful they'd been for the couple's past support, and that she hoped they could count on them in the future.

The husband drew himself up and smiled smugly.

"Actually," he said, "Gwendolyn and I were just talking about our work with you the other day. She was thinking of refreshing the sitting room, and several of the old paintings will have to go. Our children might want them, but really it would be better if we gave them to Old Art, wouldn't it, Gwen?"

The woman lowered her mask and smiled coyly. Was she trying to flirt? Bob wondered.

"They're just small things," she said. "But not without value. They should bring a tidy sum at auction. And the money would mean so much to those children." She took Gauthier's hands and pressed them firmly.

"Yes," Gauthier said. "It's a shame how little art there is in the African-American and Hispanic communities. We're just trying to do our part in the fight for equal rights for all."

What was he talking about? Bob wondered. That was complete and utter nonsense. As far as *he* knew, there was plenty of art in both the African-American and the Hispanic communities. But the couple seemed delighted to hear what Gauthier was saying.

"Anything we can do," the wife said, "to help the needy."

"Your generosity is exceeded only by your beauty, Gwen," Gauthier said. He was laying it on with a trowel, Bob saw. Even through her mask, Bob could see Mallory rolling her eyes. "When you're sure, please let us know, and we'll send a car over to pick up your generous donation. Perhaps I could take you to lunch sometime soon? Have you been to the Golden Peacock?"

So that was it, Bob thought. Modest salaries but a lavish expense account. And making sure the rich knew that they were doing their part.

As the couple wandered off, the three from Old Art grinned at one another. "That went well," Juanita Guadalupe said.

"It doesn't take much," Rémy Gauthier added. "Americans are so easy to manipulate. It was very smart of me and Giovanni to understand how susceptible Americans would be to my flattery. And it's astonishing how simple it is to make the rich feel guilty." He laughed cheerfully.

"It makes me nervous," Ricci said.

"You and your qualms!" Gauthier said. "What a great scam! To pretend that your heart bleeds for the African-Americans and the Asians and the Hispanics while you relieve the rich Americans of their goods and their money."

"We just need to keep on doing what we're doing," Guadalupe said. "Giving the grants to people no one can possibly object to. And hiring the same sorts of people as interns."

Bob felt himself getting actively angry, and for a moment he didn't think he could control it. He was afraid he'd shout or attack the three of them. If he'd only just gotten them on tape!

"I really want to *get* these guys," Bob said, startling himself with his fierceness. Mallory looked at him in surprise.

"Hold on," she said. "They sure seem dodgy, but all we have at the moment are suspicions. Though what both Worthington and Julian Jackson told us help confirm them. Still, why are you so gung ho? Did Jupiter say something?"

"No," Bob said. "It's just that − . Never mind."

He was incensed at the condescension that Gauthier and Guadalupe were exhibiting toward Americans in general − and especially by the specific way they were using minority communities by pitting people of one sort of descent against people of another. What had always made America special was that it was a place where people came together because they shared an idea – a concept of equal justice and equal opportunity for all. But both of these people – both of them immigrants themselves – were just trying to *use* that concept as a way to manipulate other human beings.

"I'm starving," Gauthier suddenly said to his partners. "Let's get some more of those crab puffs."

Bob watched them as they moved toward the food and drinks table, queuing behind the crowd that had gathered in front of it.

"I wonder why Giovanni Ricci's wife isn't with him at this party," Mallory said, as she and Bob also moved closer to the table. "With their phony talk about the African-American and Hispanic communities, I'd have thought Gauthier and Guadalupe would have seen her as a walking signboard for the cause."

"You mean because she's African-American?" Bob asked.

"Exactly," said Mallory.

Gauthier must have had his fill of crab puffs, Bob thought, for now he and his co-conspirators were talking to a middle-aged couple.

Bob and Mallory tried to get close but the crowd was thick here and it was hard to squeeze through.

"Excuse me," Bob said. "Please excuse me."

His voice was loud enough so that Giovanni Ricci looked in his direction. Bob was instantly cold, almost paralyzed. But Ricci merely smiled slightly and went back to the conversation.

"Is everything O.K., Bob?" Mallory asked. Her eyes through her raven mask glittered in the overhead light. The contrast between the deep black feathers and her bright red hair was startling.

"Sure," Bob asked, his voice a little shaky. "Why?"

"I don't know," Mallory said. "You're usually so calm, and you seem really tense."

Yeah, Bob thought, I'm really a great actor.

"No," he said. "Everything's fine. Just thinking about things."

"Anything you want to talk about?" Mallory asked.

Bob was flooded with gratitude. He knew he could talk to Mallory, and that she'd really listen, but now was obviously not the time.

"No, thanks," he said. "Not right now. We've got a job to do."

As he refocused his attention on Gauthier, Bob saw that he was still up to his tricks. He oozed insincerity. Bob was astonished that the couple he talked to didn't see right through him. Everything about him seemed false to Bob – the mannered way he gestured with his hands, the exaggerated attention he gave to what they were saying. He flattered and cajoled them. He threw back his head in stylized mirth. He was, Bob had to admit, a much better actor than Bob was. And perhaps the only reason Bob could see through his façade was because he already knew the truth.

Still, as soon as the couple they'd been talking to moved on, Gauthier began to make fun of them – of the run in the woman's stocking, the green specks of spinach from the spinach quiche caught in the man's teeth, the woman's perfume that he said reminded him of skunk cabbage. Everyone laughed.

"They're doing the same thing with everybody they meet," Mallory observed. "And they're only talking to people they think can do Old Art For Young Artists some good."

"That's why they're here," Bob said, "to

impress and butter up. To size up prospective marks. And then, when they're gone, to ridicule them."

Gauthier, Ricci, and Guadalupe were now standing close together talking, over by one of the doors that opened onto the theater's courtyard. They glanced around from time to time as if to see whether anybody was watching them. Maybe they were making a plan, Bob thought. Maybe they were going to go their separate ways so they could talk to more people than they could as a threesome. Maybe they were coming up with yet another strategy for relieving the rich of their art.

Bob and Mallory got as close as they could without being obvious – and just as they did, Giovanni's wife suddenly appeared. She had an open, welcoming face, and her long natural Afro hair had been pulled back into a bun. Bob thought she looked nice but was surprised to see that she was also pregnant.

Her husband greeted her with a hug and a kiss. "I was just coming to find you," he said. "It's time I got you home."

"I *am* a little tired," she said. "It was nice just sitting outside and breathing in the evening air. Anyway, I knew that the three of you would be promoting the foundation."

As she slipped her arm around Giovanni's waist, it was clear to Bob that she was crazy about this man she had first met when the two of them were in high school.

"The foundation!" Rémy said. "I love that word. And what a foundation it's making for all of our lives!"

"Yes, maybe," said Mrs. Ricci. "But Giovanni is so talented and I wish he'd just paint what he wants to paint, instead of working for a nonprofit." She pulled closer to her husband. "He says that after the baby is born, perhaps he'll consider it!"

"When's the baby due?" Gauthier asked. "I keep forgetting."

"In four months," Mrs. Ricci said. "But we've already got the nursery ready. And I'm going a little crazy – buying toys and watching a lot of children's films."

"Do you have strange food cravings?" Juanita Guadalupe asked – though not very sincerely, Bob thought.

"Oh, yes!" Mrs. Ricci said. "Olives and almonds." She squeezed her husband around the waist. "I really would like to go home now, Vanni."

"Of course, honey," he said, then nodded to Guadalupe and Gauthier and led his wife toward the exit.

When they were gone, Gauthier said, "I think he may be serious about quitting after the baby's born. Which would be a disaster for our future. Not that he would tell anyone what he knows – he's in too deep for that. But how would we ever find another partner with his particular talents?"

"We wouldn't," said Guadalupe. "Though if we can pull this mask stunt off, it might not even matter."

"Did the appraisal come in?" Gauthier asked.

"Yes," Guadalupe said. "The appraiser pretends he's knowledgeable, but he obviously can't tell the difference between a fake and the genuine article. The fool thinks the thing's a re-production – but if it were offered at auction at a place like Christie's or Sotheby's, it might sell for as much as five million."

Bob knew that Christie's and Sotheby's were famous auction houses, with branches and auction rooms all over the world. Sotheby's was headquartered in New York and Christie's in London.

"That's fabulous," said Gauthier. "Absolutely primo. Of course, it never *could* be auctioned at Sotheby's or Christie's, but I bet a private buyer would pay a lot for it. A *lot*. The main thing is to find a way to keep Giovanni from jumping ship until after it's sold."

"It's risky," Guadalupe said.

"Every great scheme involves some danger," Gauthier said. "But the rube is as naïve as they come – and as trusting. He'd never guess what we're up to in a million years."

Up to this moment, Bob hadn't had the slightest trouble hearing any part of this private conversation, but all of a sudden a troupe of masked revelers swept between him and Mallory and Gauthier and Guadalupe, blowing whistles and roaring with laughter. By the time they moved away again, Gauthier and Guadalupe were several steps farther along in their conversation.

While they still seemed to be talking about the risky but lucrative scheme, they were now also talking about how best to hide something – "in the meanwhile," as they put it – and as Bob and Mallory were able to hear their words again, neither of them had any idea what the something was that Gauthier and Guadalupe wanted to hide.

Now another group of revelers was making it impossible to hear the conversation – at least without getting so close they'd be in danger of getting caught.

"Did you hear anything before the 'in the meanwhile' part?" Bob asked Mallory.

"Not a word," she said. "Though I suppose they must be talking about whatever it is they think they could auction off for five million."

"I wonder what Guadalupe meant when she said that if they can pull the mask stunt off, it might not even matter if Giovanni quit the foundation," Bob said.

"I don't know," Mallory said. "But 'masking' can mean a lot of things. It can mean concealing something from view, or protecting things with sheets of plastic. As we know from the case with the falconer painting, it can also mean painting over a painting with another painting. Or simply camouflaging something. Giving it protective coloration."

"That's true," said Bob thoughtfully. "Of course, it might also have something to do with this masked ball."

"It might," Mallory said. "But I've no idea how."

Neither did Bob. As he studied the part of Gauthier's and Guadalupe's faces he could still see, he also found himself studying their masks. They were intricate, in the Venetian style, and it seemed to Bob that they had both been carefully chosen to make their wearers appear happy-go-lucky and friendly – although by now they had proven that they were anything but.

Just then, the noise around Bob and Mallory died down enough for them to hear Gauthier and Guadalupe's conversation once again. When they did, the topic seemed to be the man Gauthier had said earlier would never guess what Old Art was up to in a million years – though now Gauthier was saying that, on second thought, this man might be their biggest danger.

"It's true he's naive," he said. "But he's also clever – a lot cleverer than you might think from his accent – and once he's delivered the goods, he might put two and two together. Especially if he ends up going to the auction."

"Why would he do that?" Guadalupe said, suddenly sounding quite alarmed.

"He probably wouldn't. But if he did – " Gauthier responded.

"Yes," said Guadalupe. "If that happens, we may need to take some drastic action."

"I don't know if we could do that safely, though," said Gauthier.

"I think we could, if we had to," said Guadalupe. "Aside from his family, he knows no one in this country, and if he's found one day on a road, the victim of a hit and run, I don't think there'd be much risk to us."

Bob looked at Mallory, his eyes wide. The whole evening had been a fact-finding mission, and although he hadn't known what to expect, it seemed they'd stumbled on something a lot bigger than they'd imagined.

Luckily, as both of them stood stunned at the turn the conversation had suddenly taken, another crowd of people came between them and Gauthier and Guadalupe. This time, Bob took the opportunity to walk purposefully away.

He could feel Mallory following him, and once they were clear of the immediate area, they agreed that they should find Jupiter as soon as possible to tell him what they'd heard. Had Gauthier and Guadalupe *really* been threatening to kill someone? If so, then surely they could get them for *that,* if for nothing else, Bob thought grimly.

7

A Missed Opportunity

As he, Mallory, Pete, and Bob sat in their butterfly chairs in HQ2 the following afternoon, Jupiter no longer had any doubt that they had a case to pursue. But, so far at least, it seemed the kind of case that would take more headwork than footwork. He also couldn't help but notice that Bob was less talkative then usual, really quiet. Something was bothering him.

"Just to review," he said to Bob and Mallory. "Until Gauthier and Guadalupe began talking after Ricci left, you were mainly able to confirm what we already suspected – that Old Art For Young Artists targets racial minorities for their grants and uses that as a way to publicize what they do – and to make rich people feel guilty so they'll give more."

Bob simply nodded in response.

"That's right," Mallory said. "We also saw that Ricci and his wife seem happily married, but the other two seem more like business partners. It could have been the masks, but there was zero chemistry between them. It was only after the Riccis left that they got down to

120

brass tacks."

"And that might include murder, apparently," Jupiter said. "Though we have no idea who the intended victim might be. All we know is that he has an accent, which may mean that he's a recent immigrant. Unfortunately for us, America is full of immigrants."

"Yes," said Mallory. "Although we got another clue when they said that once he's delivered the goods, he might put two and two together – especially if he ends up going to the auction."

"Why was that a clue?" Jupiter asked.

"I got the strong impression that while they'd been talking earlier about an auction at Sotheby's or Christie's, when Gauthier mentioned an auction the second time, he meant the ones Guadalupe runs in Los Angeles."

"I agree with that," Bob said – somewhat to Jupiter's relief. "Guadalupe sounded alarmed, and since we know from Worthington that she seems to run the Old Art auctions, it was as if she was suddenly imagining a scene in her own auction room."

"I see," Jupiter said. "So whatever this man is making, it will probably be sold at an Old Art auction."

"That reminds me," Mallory said.

"We've got to get our masks back to the Costume Bank by four this afternoon."

"Yes," Jupiter said. "We don't want to have to pay for another day."

"Are things really that bad?" Pete asked.

"It depends on what you mean by bad," Jupiter said. "We're low on funds, so we'll take the masks back later today. But first, let's sum up what we know."

In a way, he thought, he'd been doing that ever since Bob and Mallory had come running up to him at the Gala the night before. They'd seemed not only excited, but upset – and in a way that proved justified when they told him what they'd overheard.

Now, he sat back in his chair and folded his hands in front of him as he lined his thoughts up. He always preferred to proceed in an orderly manner.

"We have five separate sources of information now," he said. "Worthington said he thought Old Art used a house bidder in their auctions to drive up the price. Sibyl Saskatchewan told us she thought they gave out grants not according to the principles in their mission statement but according to whom they thought would serve them best in the long run. Lyle said nothing definite, but that he had suspicions

122

about the organization, and Cornelius's great-nephew hadn't had a good experience working as an intern for them.

"Still, all of that pales in comparison to what Bob and Mallory heard − that Gauthier and Guadalupe are willing to murder a man they are currently using, if he should somehow figure out what they're up to."

"I think that about sums it up," Mallory said. "So what's your hypothesis, Jupiter?"

"I think we may conclude," Jupiter said, "and not as a hypothesis but as clearly proven fact, that Old Art for Young Artists is doing something wrong. We don't know what they're doing, but it looks like they've set up this organization as a blind − something to cover up what they're really up to, which is almost certainly against the law, and definitely not non-profit. Up until last evening, I had assumed they were embezzling, but what Bob and Mallory heard would seem to suggest something else. Though I'm not sure what, exactly. Boring as it sounds, even to me, I think we need to find out how nonprofits are regulated. Since they don't pay taxes, the government has to keep an eye on them somehow, in terms of how much money they take in."

Mallory opened up her computer and

scanned an article quickly. "It says here that all nonprofits are regulated by local, state, and federal law, and that they have to be governed by a board of directors," she said.

"What do they do?" Pete asked.

"They're legally responsible for making sure that the nonprofit does what its mission statement says it will do, that its money is handled well, and that its work is in the public interest."

"So there *is* some oversight," Jupiter said. "Can you find out who's on the Board of Directors for Old Art?" he asked.

"Sure," Mallory said. Jupiter watched as she navigated to the organization's website and clicked on Board of Directors.

"It says here that the five members of the board are – and I quote – 'prominent members of the community who give selflessly of their time so that underprivileged children might profit.'"

"Anyone we know?" Jupiter asked.

Mallory shook her head. "Not really. But Mrs. Gwendolyn Hodges is one of them."

Bob snorted. "In other words, Gauthier has the board of directors eating out of his hand."

"She was one of the people you overheard the three of them talking to?" Jupiter asked.

"Correct," said Mallory. "Gauthier flattered her shamelessly. And she just lapped it up. Some oversight.

"Hey," she added. "Look at this." She'd navigated to the home page of Old Art for Young Artists and was pointing to a new banner headline that said FLASH GRANT DAY. "It says here that Juanita Guadalupe will be at a jobs fair at the Rocky Beach City Park tomorrow, and she'll be giving out what they're calling 'mini-grants.'"

"What are those?" Pete asked.

"Cash grants of $50 and $100 to what they're calling deserving young artists under the age of 16. Don't you think someone should have been working at their art for a while and have achieved a certain level of competence before anyone goes around calling them an artist?" she asked. "And giving them money?"

Jupiter agreed but didn't say anything. "She's handing out cash?" he asked.

"It looks like it," Mallory said.

"And how many of these mini-grants is she making?" Jupiter asked.

"It doesn't say," Mallory said.

"What are the grants for?" Pete asked.

"For buying art supplies," Mallory said. "But not just paint and brushes. You can use it for ballet shoes or sheet music or printer ink and paper. Just about anything, I guess."

"It's very sly publicity," Jupiter said. "Though not inexpensive."

"It says she'll also be interviewing and hiring summer interns," Mallory said. "They have a few slots left. You have to be between 15 and 25. I wonder why that is."

"Maybe because those are the only people they can get for minimum wage," Pete said.

Jupiter shook his head in disagreement. "We've noticed that aside from Gauthier, Guadalupe, and Ricci, there are almost no older people working there. All 25 or under, and then only for three months."

"It says on the website that's because they hire young artists and they want them to have time to devote to their art," Mallory said.

Jupiter shook his head even more vigorously.

"I don't have a lot of experience in this sort of thing," he said, "but it seems logical to assume that in any company, older workers act as guardians of the company culture, and it seems to me just as odd to hire only people under 25 as it is to turn over an entire workforce every three months. The young interns don't have a clue about what's going on, and don't have time to learn before their three months are up."

He remembered the pictures of the interns on the website, perhaps taken right at the start of their tenure – bright, happy, idealistic young faces. Certainly a boon for public relations. Then he thought of what Sibyl Saskatchewan had suggested when they were renting their masks.

"Why don't we run an experiment?" he asked.

"What kind of experiment?" Pete asked.

"Why don't the four of us go to the park tomorrow afternoon and check things out?" Jupiter suggested. "If Old Art is giving away money, why don't we get some?"

"You mean we should apply for mini-grants?" Mallory asked.

"Partly," Jupiter said. "I think two of us should apply for mini-grants and two of us should apply to be summer interns."

"What?" Pete asked. "We already have part-time jobs."

"I don't mean that we should accept them," Jupiter said. "Merely that we should apply. It would be best if we could use false names, but I think that might be illegal and we want to stay on the right side of the law whenever we can. So we'll use our real names and addresses. But that should be fine. The masks we wore last night kept us anonymous, so we'll just be four more applicants who show up."

"What's the experiment?" Pete asked.

"Pete and I can apply as interns, and Mallory and Bob, you can apply for minigrants. That way we can test Ms. Saskatchewan's theory. If she's right, Mallory and I will have little chance of being successful."

"You mean you think Pete and I *will* be successful," Bob said – almost angrily, Jupiter thought. "Because of how we look, and nothing else."

"I don't like it," Pete said. "I don't want to know if I'd get the job just because my grandparents came from Mexico."

"Of course," Jupiter said, "this is not a scientific test, not at all. But it might be suggestive. And besides, it will give me a chance to assess this Juanita Guadalupe and find out everything I can about Old Art. I'll ask her as many questions as she asks me. After all, we've found out next to nothing online about the woman. It's as though she appeared out of nowhere right before she married Gauthier."

"I don't know," Bob said. "You and Mallory are good at acting, but Pete's not very good. And I'm downright terrible."

"No acting required," Jupiter said. "Pete's just himself, applying for an internship, and you're a young writer applying for a grant. Surely you could use fifty dollars to buy paper and ink."

"Well, maybe," Bob said. "If you put it that way."

Jupiter pinched his bottom lip. "And while we're making plans, I think we ought to take Julian Jackson up on his offer to introduce us to his intern friend. Now let's take our masks back to the costume bank."

The four of them buckled on their helmets and headed for downtown. When they got to the Rocky Beach Costume Bank, they found a line of people returning both costumes and masks, and Jupiter could see that the person taking them in wasn't Sibyl Saskatchewan but a woman he assumed must be her daughter Sabrina. As they stood in line, waiting to reach her, he looked around at the other customers.

To his surprise, just ahead of them he saw Peggy Thomas, the dancer Califia's mother had introduced them to the night before. She looked tired this morning. Although he himself hadn't talked to her the night before, Pete and Mallory had. When she saw the four of them standing behind her, she made a visible effort to straighten up and look more cheerful.

"Hello, again!" she called out.

"Hello," Mallory said. "I'm sorry we didn't see you again last night. We never even saw your mask."

When Peggy Thomas held it up, Jupiter saw that it was one of the Venetian masks – black and silver, studded with glass jewels and glitter, and decorated with ostrich and peacock feathers.

"Wow!" Mallory said. "That's pretty fancy."

"Yes," said Peggy. "More suitable for a ballet dancer than a dancer like me. But when I got here the other day, I was in a rush to get something, anything, and this is what I ended up with. It's been terrible not having Clay to advise me on basic things like this. I can be so indecisive."

She stepped around the one person who had been waiting between them – moving back in line. Standing next to her in normal daylight, and during a normal day, Jupiter could see that she must once have been quite beautiful and that, even now, she had a lovely face. Although he was normally not good at the sort of small talk required in a situation like this, he was flooded with sympathy and tried his best to be kind to this recently widowed woman.

"We all need advice all the time," he said.

Peggy Thomas looked at him gratefully. "I understand from Califia's mother that the four of you are detectives. Are you investigating something now? Clay loved reading murder mysteries, but I have to admit that I don't. Though I expect your investigations don't involve murders very often!"

"Not often," Jupiter said. But though he was smiling as he said it, it was disturbing to have a total stranger bring up the subject in this context. Although he had tried to seem cool and collected at the meeting in HQ2, ever since Bob and Mallory had come running up to him and Pete the night before, he'd felt quite unsettled about the news that Rémy Gauthier and Juanita Guadalupe had actually talked about committing murder.

Of course, they hadn't used that word, but it was clear from the context what they'd actually meant. Pete had suggested they make an appointment with Chief Reynolds – the police chief of Rocky Beach – to tell him what

Bob and Mallory had heard, but Jupiter had said no. Since the Gala had been noisy, the conversation had been repeatedly interrupted, and the two apparent villains had been wearing masks, there was no realistic way that Chief Reynolds would be able to take any action. Besides, no crime had been committed. Contemplating a crime was not a crime in itself.

Not that Jupiter thought Bob and Mallory had been mistaken. On the contrary, he was certain they hadn't been. Still, the circumstances of the masked surveillance had been such that an official police force would find it impossible to justify an investigation. Which meant that The Three Investigators had to find enough evidence – and quickly! – to convince even the most skeptical members of officialdom that Old Art For Young Artists was up to no good.

"What *do* you investigate?" Peggy Thomas asked as the line moved slowly forward. "I seem to remember reading an article several years ago about some young people who found a bag of gold nuggets in the floor of the Carnegie Library in Auburn. That wasn't you, by any chance?"

"Actually, it was," said Jupiter. "Our friend Hector Sebastian introduced us to a woman named Isabella Chang, and while we were investigating her ancestor, we stumbled across the path that led to the gold."

"How exciting!" Peggy Thomas said, looking genuinely impressed. "I hope she gave you a reward for your clever work!"

Pete piped up, from his place behind Jupiter. "She sure did! She gave us a 10% finder's fee! But after a couple of years, a lot of it is gone."

Peggy smiled kindly. "Money has a way of doing that. When I retired from Alvin Ailey's dance company, and Clay and I moved to California, we thought we were as rich as kings, but since both of us were lucky enough to live a long life, we had time to find out differently. The need for money never vanishes, no matter what. And now that Clay is gone, our daughter and son are urging me to move to a retirement community. But I still teach dance sometimes, so I don't think of myself as retired, and I'd rather stay where I am – in the house that Clay and I lived in so happily together for so many years."

"You still teach dance?" asked Mallory.

"I do," Peggy said. "That's how I met Sibyl and her daughter and granddaughter. Little Scarlett wants to be a dancer and goes to ballet school, but once a week she also takes lessons in modern dance. I have a dance studio in my house where I teach private students."

"Blimey!" Mallory said. "I can see why you don't want to move to a retirement community!"

"Yes," Peggy said. "Although I teach some of my students for free. Dance lessons are expensive, and there are a lot of youngsters who deserve them. Sometimes it's the children of parents who can't afford them who deserve them most."

Jupiter could tell that Pete was fighting an almost irresistible urge to say something about Old Art For Young Artists when the line ahead of Peggy Thomas suddenly came to an end. As Sabrina Saskatchewan suddenly saw the woman standing in front of her, she broke into an enormous smile. "Peggy! What are you doing here?" she asked.

"Returning a mask from last night's Gala, like everyone else," Peggy Thomas said. "I thought Sibyl would be here when I brought it back, but it's nice to see you, Sabrina!"

"It's nice to see you, too," Sabrina said. "But what do you mean, you *rented* a mask? Surely my mother didn't make you rent it after all you're doing for Scarlett?"

"Sibyl seems to think that the Costume Bank is going to go under if things don't turn around soon."

"My mother is *always* thinking that," Sabrina said. "But does this place look like it's going to go under to you?" As Peggy Thomas slid the mask and her receipt across the counter, Sabrina punched some buttons on the cash register, pulled out some bills, and handed them to the dancer.

"Sometimes I think those chopsticks my mother has taken to wearing have addled her brains," she said firmly. "I'm not going to let you pay for the rental, whatever my mother says. Not when you're giving Scarlett free lessons. Did she tell you Sabrina's ballet school didn't get the grant? No new barre, I guess."

"Oh, that's too bad," Peggy said.

"My mother was just telling me yesterday how much she disapproves of the way Old Art For Young Artists behaves."

"What do you mean?" Peggy Thomas asked as she put the bills Sabrina had given her in her purse. "I just gave them a donation last month. I thought I could use the tax break, and I liked what they told me they were doing with the money they raise."

"It *sounds* good, I guess," said Sabrina.

"But they gave a much better-off school the grant instead."

"I wish I'd known that before I made the donation," Peggy Thomas said regretfully. She turned to Jupiter and the others. "This is what I meant about it being terrible not having Clay around any more to advise me."

As she turned to leave, Jupiter couldn't resist. Though he was eager to return their masks, he stopped Peggy Thomas as she was leaving. "Forgive me for asking," he said. "But would you mind telling me what you donated to that place you were just talking about?"

"Some art Clay collected when he was part of the Harlem jazz scene. He actually didn't much like it. It was in a box in the basement when he died. I didn't think it would be worth enough for me to try to sell it for the money I could get."

"I see," Jupiter said, nodding.

And with that, Peggy Thomas was leaving and The Three Investigators were returning their masks to Sabrina. Only after they'd done that did it occur to Jupiter that he should have asked Peggy for her address and phone number – or at least should have asked her if she'd be willing to tell him more about the process by which she'd donated art to Old Art For Young

Artists.

He asked Sabrina for her address and phone number instead, and although at first she was reluctant to give it, she changed her mind when he explained that her mother had asked him and his friends to investigate Rémy Gauthier, Juanita Guadalupe, and Giovanni Ricci.

"Oh, *you're* The Three Investigators?" she said. "My mother mentioned meeting you the other day. Well, sure, then. This is Peggy's card."

Jupiter looked at the card, and when he saw that Peggy Thomas lived in the same neighborhood in Sherman Oaks as Lyle and Cornelius, he wondered whether they might be friends. He wished he could get going with interviewing her right now – and also with interviewing the friend of Julian Jackson who was working as an intern this summer. In fact, he had the funny feeling that he'd missed an opportunity when he'd let Peggy Thomas leave the Costume Bank without talking to her first.

At least he was optimistic about the Jobs Fair tomorrow. He had a scheme he planned to try out there, and even though he knew it was pointless to try to interest the police in the conversation Mallory and Bob had overheard, he was pretty certain Chief Reynolds would be intrigued by his idea – especially if it worked. And even if it didn't, he knew that Pete, at least, would love seeing it play out!

8

At The Jobs Fair

The morning of the Jobs Fair, Pete was happy to be able to spend a few hours with his parents before leaving for the city park. It had been a while since they'd eaten breakfast together, and as he ate his cereal, Pete told his parents about getting the masks at the Costume Bank and attending the Gala at the Theatre Festival – how Mallory and Bob had shadowed two men named Rémy Gauthier and Giovanni Ricci, because the woman who ran the Costume Bank had told them she thought they were shady.

"Ricci?" his father asked. "Any relation to Alyssa Ricci?"

Pete looked at his father, amazed. "She's his wife. Do you know her?"

"Not well," his father said. "But I've worked with her. She's a set designer. A lovely woman. She grew up in Los Angeles. She told me she'd been in love with this Italian guy who left to go back to Italy with his father just before his junior year of high school. They wound up staying for quite some time. When he finally came back to the States, he and Alyssa found each other again and got married. And now she's having a baby! She's over the moon."

"That's what I heard," Pete said. "I've never seen her myself, but Bob and Mallory did. She was at the Gala with her husband."

"She's crazy about the guy," Pete's father said. "I hope he's not in any real trouble. She told me that he was a really good artist – a *great* artist she actually said – and that she wished he'd just trust his talent and get out of the foundation he worked for. She said it wasn't good for him."

"No," Pete said. "I don't think it is."

"So finish your story," his mother said.

"So far, that's all there is," Pete said. "But today the four of us are going to a Jobs Fair at the city park to apply for jobs and grants and stuff – not really, but just to see if this Old Art place would really hire us. Or give us money. Jupe's idea is that he and I will try competing for the same job."

"Oh, dear," said his mother. She looked sympathetic.

His father smiled a bit uneasily. "You know how much I admire your competitive spirit, son. But don't you think you should give that particular competition a miss?"

"I can't," he said. "It's Jupiter's idea that Old Art is a blind for some sort of criminal activity, and that the way they cover it up is by hiring and giving grants to minorities. There are so many Hispanics in California that it seems weird to think anyone would see me as part of a minority, but, well —"

"So you and Bob are the test case?" Pete's father said, smiling broadly. "Sacrificial goats? Though Bob is a slightly smaller goat than you are!"

"Oh, don't put it that way, Martín!" said Pete's mother. "This isn't ancient Greece!"

"No," his father said. "But whatever happened to the idea that God loves all his children equally? So the theory is that you and Jupiter will apply for the same job and that you'll be the one to get it, because of your family background?"

"Bingo," Pete said. "But even in a fake competition and as part of an investigation, that feels wrong. I mean, if I was in a contest with Jupe that involved throwing a ball, or head-butting some bad guys, or getting along with children or animals — or even cheering up someone if they were gloomy — I'd win hands down. But when it comes to a job at a place that deals with art, and handles money, Jupiter would win, every time."

"Oh, Pete," his mother said, bending over to kiss his cheek. "It's a strange world sometimes, but even if I never did anything else in my life, I could die happy knowing I had you as a son!"

Although his mother often said nice things to Pete, this was one of the nicest things he could ever remember.

In fact, even an hour later, as he, Bob, Mallory and Jupiter pedaled their bikes into the Rocky Beach City Park, he was still feeling good about her comment.

The Jobs Fair was in the pavilion, and unlike a lot of the other young people in attendance, Pete and his friends had gotten a bit dressed up. Pete and Bob wore neat short-sleeved button-down shirts and freshly laundered jeans.

Jupiter was wearing his more or less standard uniform – a long-sleeved button-down shirt with the sleeves rolled up and a pair of pressed khakis – while Mallory wore a pair of white cargo pants and a teal V-neck top with three-quarter sleeves. In a sane world, Pete thought, all *four* of them would have stood out as likely job candidates, and he hoped Jupiter would be wrong.

"Let's go over the plan one more time," Jupiter said. "We shouldn't act like we're together or even particularly know one another – we're just four kids who showed up at about the same time to apply for the grants and internships. Of course, we're taking a calculated risk by using our own names, so we should minimize the risk in every other way we can."

"How?" Pete asked.

"If there ever was a time to gather information and not divulge it," Jupiter said, "it's today. Don't be chatty, even if you get nervous."

Uh, oh, Pete thought. That was exactly what happened when he got nervous.

"I expect there'll be applications they want us to fill out," Jupiter said, "so if nothing comes of the interview, do everything you can to take any papers you've filled out away with you. No paper trail. Just thank Ms. Guadalupe and leave. If something does come of the interview, then it may be impossible to grab the application. But do the best you can. Ready?"

They all nodded grimly as if they were about to take a math exam. At least that's the way Pete felt. Together they wandered over toward the pavilion. Already it was crowded. The picnic tables that were usually jammed together under the slightly-slanted green metal roof had been moved out onto the grass surrounding the large rectangular concrete pad. So many booths had been set up inside that a number of them spilled beyond the pavilion.

Some of the booths advertised volunteer work and others promoted vocational jobs – construction, plumbing, trucking, auto repair. The city park itself was hiring grounds-keepers and people to run the concession stand. They passed a team from Rocky Beach Community College advertising its IT programs. In the back on the right hand side, next to a booth from a cosmetology school called XTreme Beauty, they found Old Art's booth.

"O.K., Jupiter said, keeping his voice low. "One at a time, and let some other people go between us."

Pete stepped forward bravely. Juanita Guadalupe sat behind a small table, flanked by two standing teenagers, one Asian and one Hispanic. Pete assumed they must be interns who'd already been hired.

When he looked at them inquiringly, the Asian girl said, "Are you here for the mini-grant or the internship?"

For a moment, Pete froze, unable to re-member which he was supposed to apply for, and then he stammered, "The – the internship."

"Here's the application form," she said, grabbing a page from the bottom of the pile she held. "Just fill it out and come back for the interview. And here's a pencil."

"Thanks," Pete said. Glancing behind him, he saw that Jupiter was now talking to the other intern. Bob and Mallory had split up and were standing nearby, waiting for their chance.

Pete found a picnic table that was partially shaded and sat down to look at the application. He was surprised when Jupiter joined him, sitting on the far end on the opposite side. "I thought you said we were supposed to pretend we didn't know each other," Pete said.

"I'm just sitting here," Jupiter said. "I could be anyone." He turned his attention to the paper he'd been given, and so did Pete. He read quickly down the information the application asked for.

He was puzzled that there were no questions about what experience he had – such as being a volunteer at the Animal Rescue Center – or what skills he might bring to the job of an intern. Nothing about his ambitions or life plans. Just a question about why he wanted the job – and whether or not he had an art form.

"Why do I want the job?" he hissed at Jupiter.

"Because you need the money and you want to help disadvantaged children," Jupiter said quietly.

"Oh," Pete said. "And by the way, what's your art form?"

Jupiter smiled at him wryly. "It really doesn't matter, because I won't be taking the job even if it's offered to me. What do you think I should write down?"

"How about print making?" Pete suggested. "Remember when you made those ink prints of your feet?"

Jupiter laughed. "Great idea." He wrote on his application.

Pete went back to the form. He put his art form down as wood carving – by which he meant whittling – then entered his name, address, phone number, e-mail, and birthplace.

He paused when he got to *ethnicity* and rolled his eyes. Here we go, he thought. Was asking that question even legal on a job application? He wrote down 'American.'

Are your parents married? Parents' Name(s). Number of Siblings, Number of Bedrooms. Wait a minute, Pete thought.

"What's with the nosy questions?" he

hissed at Jupiter. "Why do they want to know if my parents are married? And what's this with the number of bedrooms?"

"It's a way of judging how wealthy your parents are," Jupiter said.

"Well, at least they won't be able to tell us apart," Pete said. "We both have no siblings, and we both have three bedrooms, and our parents were married, and – "

"That's good," Jupiter said. "Are you finished? Let's go get in line. You should go first."

Waiting to be interviewed, Pete recognized the girl talking to Ms. Guadalupe from school.

He didn't know her – had never even talked to her – but he was sure she'd just graduated. She had long blond hair and seemed very eager, but after talking for a few minutes, she stood up looking disappointed. "Sorry," the woman said. "I don't think you have the skills we're looking for at the moment."

What skills? Pete wondered. There was nothing on the sheet about that. All the stuff that Jupiter was good at ought to have shown up on the application form, but nowhere on that piece of paper had Jupiter been allowed to stand out.

As he took a seat, Juanita Guadalupe perused his application form, then looked up at him and smiled. "Hello, Pete," she said. "Or should I say 'Hola, Pedro'?"

"Pete's fine," he said.

She asked him some questions about what else he was studying in school, and what his parents did for a living, and what he wanted to do with his life. She ended by asking, "Can you tell me anything about why you want to work for Old Art?"

"It … it looks interesting," Pete said.

"And it says here you're a wood carver. What do you carve?"

"Just – stuff," Pete said, embarrassed. "I'm still trying things out."

"That's wonderful," Juanita Guadalupe said. "Well, I think we may be able to use you. You look like you're strong enough for warehouse work. How would that suit you?"

"Wow," Pete said. "Just like that? Gee, thanks. But I haven't actually asked my parents yet if I can do this. I didn't expect – Do you have a card so that I can call you after I talk to them?"

"Sure," Juanita Guadalupe said. She reached in a shoulder bag she'd slung over the back of the chair and brought out a business card with Old Art's number on it. "You can leave me a message here. But call as soon as you can. Otherwise I'll offer the internship to someone else."

"Thanks!" Pete said. He stood, deftly picking up his application papers. "I will."

He casually walked away, feeling very proud of himself for having evaded the job and also for getting away with his application. He nodded to Jupiter, who'd been watching from a safe distance.

There was no one else waiting, so Jupiter walked up and took the seat Pete had just vacated. "Hello," Pete heard him say.

Jupiter's interview was even shorter than Pete's had been. In no time, Jupiter got up and shook the woman's hand. As he approached, Pete could see that he too had managed to grab his application. He slipped it very carefully into a large manila envelope.

"Well?" Pete asked.

Jupiter shook his head.

"She turned you down?" Pete asked, outraged. "Why?"

"She didn't say," Jupiter said. "She told me my application was most interesting, but that I didn't fit who they were looking for at the moment."

"And who are they looking for?" Pete asked. He couldn't believe how heated he felt. "She offered me the job but turned you down?"

"What did she say to you?" Jupiter asked.

"She said I looked strong and could work in the warehouse."

"There you go," Jupiter said. "That's better than 'You're Hispanic.'"

"In what world does this happen?" Pete said.

"In this one, apparently," Jupiter told him. "Of course it's not a scientific test. We'd need lots more data for it even to start to qualify. But it is suggestive. Come on. Let's go sit down and wait for Bob and Mallory."

He led the way to one of the tree-shaded picnic tables. Pete was still fuming, but Jupiter seemed quite calm. "You look almost happy," Pete said. "What's with the manila envelope?"

"Just another small experiment," Jupiter said. "Which I think worked out pretty well. But I'll save the explanation until Bob and Mallory can hear about it too."

Geez, Pete thought. Another mystery!

Bob and Mallory had hung back while

Jupiter and Pete got their applications from the Old Art booth, but as soon as they'd left the pavilion, first Bob and then Mallory had said they wanted to apply for a mini-grant and were given the proper paperwork. Now they sat at a picnic table not far from the one where Jupiter and Pete sat.

"This is weird," Bob said. "Don't you think?"

Mallory, who had been studying the application, looked up and smiled at him. "Sort of," she said. "But it's interesting."

Bob looked down at the paper before him. After all the identifying information — *name, address, e-mail, phone* — the questions focused on the purpose of the grant. Old Art wanted to know what your art form was, when you became interested in it, and what specifically you'd use the money for.

Those were easy, Bob thought. He wrote down that his art form was narrative nonfiction, that he'd been interested in writing since 6th grade. He wasn't sure what to put down for how he'd use the money, so he left it blank.

"What are you going to say your art form is?" he asked Mallory.

"Hmm," Mallory said. "I could say I was interested in architecture, but I was thinking that maybe it would be good if I just said writing. Like you. That way our applications would be pretty identical."

"That's a good point," Bob said. "But maybe they'd want to give grants to different art forms and you'd have a better chance with architecture." They talked about the pros and cons of each for a few minutes and decided that Mallory should apply as a writer. That would help level the playing field.

Bob went back to his application. Further down on the page he found a bunch of intrusive questions that had nothing to do with art but seemed to be about how badly the applicant needed the grant. Old Art wanted to know his parents' names and careers and whether they owned their house or were renters. There was a space for him to enter their yearly income, if he knew it.

Bob was flooded with embarrassment. So much for making their applications identical. Both his parents had full-time jobs and made good salaries – though he didn't know exactly how much they made. They also owned the house they lived in.

Mallory, on the other hand, had a single mother and the two of them lived in a rented apartment in the Wessex House. Mallory's mother's work in costume design was boom-or-bust. She was part of the gig economy and had to work hard to land whatever movie jobs she got. Bob's parents and he had health insurance and other benefits, while Mrs. MacLeod had none. He knew Mallory didn't feel sorry for herself in any way, but he suddenly felt almost guilty. If they had really been applying for these grants, she would have deserved one a whole lot more than he did.

He felt quite uncomfortable, even squirmy, but none of this seemed to have even registered with Mallory. She kept commenting on how interested she'd be to see how all this panned out.

"So I think we should apply for the same grant, exactly," she said. "How much?"

"Seventy-five dollars sounds about right," Bob said, "given the cost of ink cartridges."

"So that's what I should put down?" Mallory asked.

"Yeah," Bob said. "Ink cartridges and paper. We can say we want to print out our writing and edit it on paper. You could also put down a notebook or two if you wanted. Why don't we do that?"

Once they'd finished their applications,

they walked together back under the pavilion's roof. It was dim after the glare of the noonday sun, and it took Bob's eyes a minute to adjust. One of the interns had wandered off, but the other, looking bored, stood idly to the side of where Juanita Guadalupe sat.

"You go first," Bob said. "I'll hang back."

He watched as Mallory took a seat opposite the woman. Ms. Guadalupe leaned forward earnestly, as though she were taking a special interest in Mallory. The remaining intern, the one who'd given Bob and Mallory the paperwork, leaned down and whispered something to Ms. Guadalupe and then sauntered away. Mallory and the woman seemed to talk for quite a while, and then Mallory stood up, turned, and walked toward Bob. As she approached, he raised his eyebrows in question and she, very subtly, shook her head no. She had a faint smile on her face as she walked past Bob, seemingly without recognizing him.

O.K., he thought, it was crunch time.

He sat down opposite Ms. Guadalupe and looked at her carefully. She wore no makeup today and her lips looked thin and pale.

"Let's see," she said, studying his application. "Another writer, I see."

"What do you mean?" Bob asked, suddenly concerned that he and Mallory had made the wrong decision. "Is that a problem?"

"Oh, no," the woman said. "It's just that I've had a good number of writing applications today. Could you tell me what you mean by narrative nonfiction?"

Bob had written that down as a description of the case reports he wrote up for the Three Investigators, and now he was cornered.

"Oh," he said, glad he wasn't Pete, who would have turned bright red under the circumstances. "I – I really didn't know what to put down. Most of my writing is about my life and what I – what I do with my friends."

"I see," Ms. Guadalupe said. "You make stories out of what happens to you."

"Sort of," Bob said, and then realized she was throwing him a lifeline. "Yes. That's it."

"Your mother's an evolutionary biologist?" she said.

"That's right," Bob said. "She teaches at Reedmore College. Here in Rocky Beach."

"And your father's a journalist."

"For the Los Angeles *Sun*," Bob said. "You know, the more I think about it, the more this seems like a mistake."

"Why do you say that?" Ms. Guadalupe asked.

"I mean, my parents are both professionals and make good money, and I have a part-time job and can afford my own ink cartridges. You should give the money to someone who needs it more."

"But wouldn't it be nice to be recognized with a grant?" the woman asked.

"I don't understand," Bob said. "Recognized how? You haven't read any of my writing."

"The world needs more Asian writers," Ms. Guadalupe said. "Don't you think?"

"But I'm not an Asian writer," Bob said. "I'm just a writer."

"I don't think you're taking yourself seriously enough," Ms. Guadalupe said. "You really deserve this money." She reached into a small metal box on the table and took out a stack of bills. She counted out three crisp $20s and three $5s and pushed them across the table at Bob.

He sat there, stunned.

"All you need to do is sign this receipt," Ms. Guadalupe said, pushing a sheet of paper at him, "and let us take your picture for our website."

Bob had a sudden adrenaline rush, and he stood up so abruptly he almost knocked over the chair he'd been sitting in.

"No," he said. "No, thank you. I've changed my mind about applying." He couldn't believe how obvious the woman had been – how blatant the scam was. It was almost as though she'd winked at him, letting him in on a secret.

She looked quite startled as he backed away and then hurried to join the others out in the field. He walked quickly, filled with anger. He thought about Mallory, or someone like her, someone who really could have used the grant and who had come to the fair, hopeful about what the money would let her do, and who had probably been turned down because of how she looked – something she had absolutely no control over and that meant next to nothing.

It was outrageous that someone like him, who didn't need the money, would be offered it anyway because then he could be a pawn in the insidious game that Old Art was playing.

It made him worse than angry. It made him sick. These people actually *were* using racial and ethnic backgrounds to divide people and set them against one another in a big ugly game of King of the Mountain. It was an awful, nasty view of the world, and it had to stop.

Pete, Mallory, and Jupiter were waiting for him.

"What's wrong?" Pete said. "You look like you're about to pop!"

"I am!" Bob said. "They gave me the grant. Ms. Guadalupe counted out seventy-five dollars in cash and shoved it at me."

"Did you take it?" Pete asked.

"Of course not," Bob said. "She wanted me to sign something and have my picture taken. She called me an Asian writer."

"Wow," Mallory said. "That's a bit blatant. Especially because you aren't. If you want to be technical about it, you're a biracial American writer – and a really good one!"

Bob could hardly believe how upset he was. After all, this was what they'd been expecting, going in.

Still, somehow until he experienced discrimination like this first-hand, he hadn't known just how angry it would make him to be judged on the way he looked on the outside, and not for who he actually was – even if the discrimination was in his favor.

"And Guadalupe offered me a job," Pete

said, "but not Jupe. Can you believe it?"

"What did you say when she made the offer?" Bob asked.

"I said I had to ask my parents first," Pete said. "I don't know where that came from, but I was pretty proud."

"Quite clever," Jupiter said.

"And I just grabbed my application and got out of there," Pete said.

Bob's stomach sank. In the rush of emotion he'd had at the end of the interview, he'd completely forgotten about grabbing the paperwork.

"Oh no," he said. "I'm sorry! I forgot. Ms. Guadalupe still has my application. Should I go back and ask for it?"

"I think that's a bad idea," Jupiter said. "You'll just draw more attention to it."

"Did the rest of you all remember?" Everyone nodded and Bob felt even more embarrassed and upset.

"But you said you didn't want the grant," Pete said. "Maybe she'll just throw away the application."

"I wouldn't worry about it," Mallory said. "What matters is that we found out what we needed to. Jupiter can say all he wants to that this wasn't a scientific test, but it seems pretty scientific to me."

That made Bob feel a little better, but he still felt angry at himself, as well as at the situation.

"That may be true, but how do we prove to the authorities what they're actually up to?" he asked.

Jupiter smiled. "I may have devised a way to get their attention," he said. He held up a manila envelope. "My application papers. And unless I'm very much mistaken, I managed to get Juanita Guadalupe to leave a very clean set of fingerprints on it."

"So that's why you put the papers in the envelope!" Pete said. "I couldn't figure it out!"

Jupiter nodded. "Ever since we did research on Gauthier, Ricci, and Guadalupe, it's bothered me that there was so little about Juanita Guadalupe online. As soon as we get back to the Salvage Yard, I'm going to call Chief Reynolds and ask if he'd be willing to run a set of fingerprints though the police database."

"I'm sure he will," said Pete. "And when he does, maybe we'll find out that Juanita Guadalupe is a murderer!"

"I don't know whether to hope for that particular thing or not," Jupiter said. "But I'm hoping we'll find out *something*. And I imagine

that if Bob has *his* way, whatever we find out
will at least be enough to get Guadalupe arrested, without any further delay!"

Jupe had certainly gotten *that* right! Bob
thought.

9

A Very Interesting Photograph

Mallory stared at Jupiter in amazement, wondering why neither she nor Bob nor Pete had thought of doing something that seemed so obvious in retrospect. That was often the way of things, though – that Jupiter was a step ahead of the rest of them. And it was certainly funny to think that while Juanita Guadalupe was turning Jupiter Jones down for a minimum wage job, he was calmly getting a set of her fingerprints!

However, all she said was, "But how can you be sure the fingerprints didn't get smudged?"

"I can't be," Jupiter said. "But I wiped the paper carefully before I wrote on it and then made certain to touch it only at the very bottom. I handed it over with the top facing her and I watched carefully the whole time. She never touched it again in the same place, so there's a very good chance a set of her prints is on the top. When Chief Reynolds's men dust it, we'll know. If we get back to the Salvage Yard quickly enough, maybe they'll even be able to do it today. Although, since it's Sunday, maybe not. Anyway, we might as well get going."

He stood up, but as Mallory did, too, she saw an all-too-recognizable figure approach the pavilion.

"Wait a minute," she said. "Speak of the devil. Don't all of you look at once. It's Rémy Gauthier." He was walking rapidly toward the Old Art booth. He oozed an insincere charm, Mallory thought, but because of his dashing Gallic looks, he also seemed to turn female heads. In fact, when Mallory saw how many girls and women looked at him with admiration, she felt more and more certain that his marriage to Juanita was a marriage of convenience.

"Listen," she said. "You guys sit tight. I won't be long."

"What are you going to do?" Pete asked.

"Eavesdrop again," Mallory said. "I think I'll pick up a brochure at the Xtreme Beauty booth. It's right next to Old Art."

Without waiting to be dissuaded, she started back toward the pavilion and got to the cosmetology booth not long after Gauthier had reached his wife. Now he stood to her left, his hand on her shoulder, bending over to get closer to her ear.

"Hello," the older woman at the XTreme Beauty booth said in a loud voice. "What beautiful hair you have! Are you thinking about a career in cosmetology?" Gauthier straightened up and glanced in her direction.

"Maybe," Mallory said. She peeked at Gauthier. He was staring at the woman with distaste. As she watched, he glanced at her briefly, as if considering whether she indeed had beautiful hair, then turned back to his wife.

Mallory's heart was beating faster as she picked up a small brochure from the table. "May I take this?" she asked.

"Certainly," the woman said. "Do you have any questions?"

"Let me just think," Mallory said, closing her eyes as if concentrating while she strained to hear the conversation over at the other booth.

"How's it going?" Gauthier asked. "I hope you're not giving out too much money."

"No," Guadalupe said. "In fact I offered $75 to some Asian kid – well, part-Asian, I guess, since his last name was Andrews – and he walked away in a huff, very rudely."

"Andrews?" said Gauthier. "The other day I gave an interview to a journalist named

164

Malcolm Andrews. He wasn't Asian, but I wonder if this kid might have been his son."

"I bet he was!" said Juanita Guadalupe, looking outraged. "He told me very smugly that his father was a journalist."

Grabbing her phone, she punched some words into a search engine and then started almost sputtering. "And get this! The kid is actually a member of some kid-sized investigative firm called The Three Investigators!"

"That's bad," said Gauthier. "I never should have agreed to be interviewed by someone I hadn't thoroughly vetted. He must have applied for the grant because his father sent him to spy on us."

Though Mallory wished she could listen to more of this conversation, she knew that every instant she stood there she was risking being noticed. So she just said to the woman running the booth, "No questions. Thanks for this." She stuffed the brochure under her arm, rejoined the boys, and said, "Let's get out of here. Fast."

Although all three of them looked at her inquisitively, she just shook her head until they were safely on their bikes and out of the far side of the park. Then she waved to everyone to stop.

"You're not going to like this," she said, "but Guadalupe and Gauthier know who we are. Or at least they know who Bob is. I heard Gauthier say that Bob's father interviewed him for the Los Angeles *Sun*. You didn't tell us he'd done that, Bob."

"I didn't know," Bob said, looking stricken. "The other morning, Dad told me he was writing an article about a local nonprofit, but he never told me the name of the place, or the name of the man he was going to interview."

Mallory looked at Bob sympathetically. "The problem is, Juanita Guadalupe remembered that you'd said your father was a journalist. When Gauthier told her he'd been interviewed by Malcolm Andrews, it didn't take long for them to confirm you were his son. Even worse, that you're a member of what she called a kid-sized investigative firm called The Three Investigators!"

"Oh, no," Pete said. "This isn't good. And not just for us. For your father, too."

"That's true," Bob said, looking even more alarmed. "Dad implied that his editor admired what this nonprofit was up to, and if Rémy Gauthier calls him up and complains about Dad supposedly having sicced me on the foundation, Dad might be taken off the story. He might even lose his job!"

Bob looked at Jupiter. Although Jupiter looked grave, he said, as reassuringly as possible, "Don't worry, Records. If Gauthier called your father's editor and said he had reason to think that your father had sent you to spy on Old Art, it might put him in an awkward position. But it would be easy enough to prove that wasn't actually what had happened."

"To prove that, we'd have to tell the editor how we got on the case to begin with," Pete said. "And if we did, I don't see how we could ever get the goods on these crooks!"

Just then, Mallory's cell phone buzzed. She answered it, even though she didn't recognize the number.

"Is that Mallory MacLeod?" said a vaguely familiar voice. "This is Julian Jackson, Cornelius Patterson's great-nephew."

"It's Julian Jackson!" she said to the others.

"How great!" she said to Julian. "I was hoping you'd call. Did you run into your friend Randy at the Farmer's Market?"

"We're still here right now," Julian said. "But I was thinking that maybe we should come to Rocky Beach to see you. We've sold everything we're going to sell today, and Randy has a pretty peculiar story about something that happened at Old Art. I thought you might be interested in it."

"Please come!" Mallory said. "We're at the city park right now, but we'll be back at the Salvage Yard in fifteen minutes. That's where our Headquarters is. In the middle of Jupiter's aunt and uncle's Salvage Yard."

"I know," Julian said. "When we got back from the Gala, Lyle and Uncle Cornelius showed me the pictures you'd sent, and I asked for your address. We'll pack up our booths and drive over there now."

"That'll be great," Mallory said. "See you soon!" She slipped her cell phone back in her pocket, then smiled broadly at the boys.

"I like this guy," she said. "He called when he said he would, his friend has a peculiar story about something that happened at Old Art, and he asked his Uncle Cornelius for our address."

Although Mallory could see that Bob was still worried about their cover being blown – and maybe even more worried that his father might be taken off his feature story – since there was nothing they could do about the problem at the moment, even Bob put all his energy into bicycling back to the Salvage Yard.

There, Mallory was happy to see that Julian and Randy hadn't yet arrived. This gave the four of them time to tidy up before they had their first official guests – who pulled up, very unexpectedly, in a souped-up muscle car.

Though Mallory knew very little about such cars, Pete was an expert, and the first ten minutes of Julian and Randy's visit was devoted to a detailed analysis of Randy's Dodge Challenger.

A short, intense-looking young man with what Mallory thought of as classic California surfer looks, Randy kept tossing his sun-bleached blond hair out of his eyes as he jabbed his finger toward one or another feature of his car. While this went on, Mallory started to doubt that he would have anything interesting to tell The Three Investigators, but as soon as the car was behind him, and he and Julian were walking into Headquarters, everything changed.

"What a dope building!" Randy said. "Way cool."

"That sign over the door is awesome," Julian said.

"Mallory designed all that," Jupiter said.

"Wow!" said Julian. "She's got real

talent.”

“Can I get you guys a drink?” Pete asked. “We have soda and juice.”

“Not right now, thanks,” Julian said. “We should get started – because you’re really not going to believe what Randy told me.”

As they all settled down on the sofa and easy chairs in the formal “visitor’s” section of their new Headquarters, Mallory was proud of how grown-up Pete and Bob and Jupiter looked. Ever since the scene in the park, Mallory had been wondering whether Jupiter might be feeling a little hurt at having been turned down for a job with Old Art. She herself hadn’t felt that way, but when she considered the high probability that Jupiter had never before tried to convince someone else to let him use his brain and his skills on their behalf and been turned down, she had to think that it had stung a bit.

On the other hand, he was probably quite pleased to discover his hypothesis had been correct. As Julian and Randy looked at one another, Jupiter asked, “Which one of you wants to start?”

“It’s really Randy’s story,” Julian said. “But even so, I’ll start. One of the things I thought was weird about Old Art when I worked there was that, although one of my main jobs was to catalogue the stuff people donated so that they could be listed as ready for auction, I was never given a copy of the original paperwork."

"The original paperwork meaning a copy of the receipt given to donors when they donate a valuable piece," Randy clarified. "I'd noticed that, too, but I hadn't really thought about how odd it was until Julian mentioned you were looking into Old Art to see if they might be bent. They say the reason is that all donations are anonymous. There's a lot of b.s. on the website about how a donor might feel embarrassed or self-conscious about the size or type of contribution if the donation wasn't anonymous."

"I remember that," Jupiter said. "They also said something about keeping the focus on the young people who get the grants."

"That's right," Julian said. "But they also encourage all the donors to get a proper appraisal, so that they can take a tax write-off when they donate. Sometimes the items are left at the warehouse before the appraisal comes through, but all the items are appraised before they go on the auction block."

"And while the directors could easily give

the interns those appraisals so that we could put together the auction catalogues, instead they have us do our own research online, and come up with our own estimates," Randy said intensely.

"All they'd really have to do to keep the donors anonymous would be to black out their names on the official appraisals," Julian added. "Instead, a bunch of untrained interns are guessing what each item is worth, just by looking at pictures on the Internet."

"To tell you the truth," Randy said, "we can't figure out why this is good for the directors — since whatever the appraisal might be, it's the bidders at the auction who decide what to pay for anything. But it seems shady enough so that we thought we should mention it."

As the two of them had been talking, tossing the explanation back and forth between them, Mallory had noticed that Jupiter was pinching his lip — always a sign that he was deeply engrossed in thought. Now he said, "That's very interesting. But I gather from what Mallory told me that you also have a more specific story to tell us."

"That's right," Randy said. "I do. I actually don't work in the warehouse myself, but I know some of the peeps who do, and I'm tight with a chick whose job it is to keep bugs – ants and wasps and bees – out of the warehouse. She doesn't mess with the donations but she's got eyes, and she notices what's been donated. If she thinks something's interesting or pretty she sometimes takes pictures with her cell phone.

"Well, about a week ago, she noticed a donation of what she thought had to be African masks. She knows I'm studying the history of the avant-garde in Paris in the early twentieth century, so she took a couple of pictures to show me."

Randy took his cell phone out of his pocket, swiped it this way and that, then held up a picture that showed some brightly colored wooden masks, most of them striped with orange and red and green.

He swiped his phone again, and Mallory could see that the second picture showed some different but similar masks – with one exception. At the far end of the row of masks was a white one.   Because of the way Randy's friend had held her cell phone, the white mask was a bit blurred, and part of it has been cut out of the frame.

Still, from what Mallory could see, the white mask was really *very* different from the others. Though it, too, seemed to be made of wood, it was about two feet long, with a wide forehead and a narrow chin. It had small narrow slits for eyes, and a long rectangular nose. From what Mallory could tell, it might come to the bottom of your rib cage if you held it in front of your face.

To her, it looked like a death mask – but even more strikingly, it looked like a piece by the artist who'd come to her attention because Rémy Gauthier had discovered a possible painting by him in a Parisian shop.

"That mask on the right looks a bit like a Modigliani," she said. "I mean, part of it is cut off, but you can see how stylized the elongation is."

Both Julian and Randy whooped with approval, and Julian said to his friend, "I told you she'd notice!" Turning to her, he said, "My uncle told me that you'd just discovered Modigliani."

"He first went to Paris in 1906," Randy said, "and he saw African masks like that there."

"You mean Modigliani?" Mallory asked.

"Absolutely," Randy said, nodding. "You really can't overestimate the influence tribal African art had on the avant-garde, particularly

Modigliani and Picasso. Still, the important thing about the story isn't that a mask like this once influenced Modigliani. It's that it's very different from the others. From my friend's pictures, it looks to me like the highly colored masks include a Chokwe mask from the Democratic Republic of Congo and a Dan mask from the Ivory Coast. But the white one basically has to be a reproduction of something called a Fang Ngil mask."

"What's that?" Pete asked.

"They're not being made any more," Randy said, "but up until the French invaded and colonized Gabon and Cameroon in the early 1900s, the masks were made by members of the Fang tribe, and worn by a male secret society called the Ngil. For hundreds of years the society ruled the Fang as a combination priesthood, police force, and court of law. They only appeared at night − wearing these terrifying white masks."

"Yes," Julian said. "People thought the masks were the ghosts of their ancestors. If you broke the laws of the Fang, you could expect the Ngil to show up at your hut − by torchlight or firelight − wearing these chalky white masks and a costume of raffia that covered the rest of them. Cornelius and Lyle actually have a reproduction of a Fang Ngil mask in their laundry room – or not a reproduction, an imitation – that they bought at a street fair one day, as a joke.

"Lyle says it's to scare him into doing laundry," Julian added. "But the Ngil really did use fear as a means of social control, and in my opinion, their masks would have scared the pants off anyone who saw them. No wonder the French invaders banned the Ngil and forbade the making of any more masks!"

"And because they forbade them," Randy said, "the masks became rarer and rarer as the years went on. They're now the holy grail of African art. A perfect Fang Ngil mask sold in 2003 for over five million dollars. It was one of only twelve or thirteen left in the whole entire world."

"Yikes!" Pete exclaimed. "Five million dollars?"

"Yes," Randy said. "Of course a reproduction would be worth a lot less. I'm not actually sure how much it *would* be worth. I'd have liked to see what the one Hazel photographed brought at the auction, but it seems I'm not going to get the chance."

"Why not?" Pete asked.

"Because after Hazel sent me these pictures, I asked her if she'd be willing to get me a better shot of the Fang Ngil reproduction," Randy said. "The last time she was in the warehouse, she tried to do it. But although all of the other masks were still just where she'd left them, the white mask was gone!"

10

Jupiter Remembers What He's Forgotten

Later, as Jupiter thought back on the moment when Randy Foreman sat in Headquarters and announced that a reproduction Fang Ngil mask was missing from the warehouse of Old Art For Young Artists, he couldn't quite understand why he had immediately felt certain that the mask hadn't been a reproduction at all, but the real thing.

After all, Randy had told them that, after the Ngil had been banned by the French, the masks had become rarer and rarer and that there were only twelve or thirteen left in the world.

Jupiter later remembered looking at Randy and thinking, "Twelve or thirteen that collectors and art historians actually *know* about!"

He also remembered feeling certain that somewhere in his overcrowded brain, he'd already tucked a piece of relevant information that he couldn't quite locate now.

But while this was frustrating, it was almost completely overshadowed by the sense that what had begun as a rather unexciting investigation − one in which he and his friends had known right from the start who the bad guys were − had suddenly become of pressing interest. It was always a wonder when a rare piece of history was tossed up from the past into the present.

In the course of The Three Investigators' last twelve cases, this had happened a total of five times. Each case had been different, but in each, the excitement of helping return to the world something old and either unique or highly unusual had been pretty big.

Up to this moment, none of his friends had said much of anything in response to the punch line of Randy's story, but now both Mallory and Bob started talking at once, and, perhaps not surprisingly, they suggested just what Jupiter had thought − that the mask might be the real thing.

Their reasons, however, were different from his. While Jupiter was certain that he had met someone who had said or done something that had to do with the theft of the mask, Bob and Mallory both knew perfectly well why they had leapt to the conclusion that they had.

"At the Gala," Mallory said, "when we

were spying on Rémy Gauthier and Juanita Guadalupe, we overheard them say that some appraiser they had hired couldn't tell the difference between a fake and the genuine article."

Bob added, "And Juanita Guadalupe said that if they could pull off what she called 'this mask stunt,' it might not matter if Giovanni Ricci quit the foundation. Now that we know about these African masks, well..."

Both Julian and Randy were looking at Bob with a dawning excitement.

"You're kidding!" Randy said, shaking his hair out of his eyes. "They really talked about a mask stunt? And about an appraiser not being able to tell the difference between a fake and the genuine article?"

"Not only that," said Mallory. "Juanita Guadalupe said something about how if what they were talking about were offered at an important auction house, it might sell for as much as five million dollars.' That's quite a coincidence, given what you told us about that other Fang Ngil mask!"

"But how are they going to sell it?" Pete asked. "And how did *they* know it was real if even a regular appraiser didn't?"

"I think I can answer that," Jupiter said. "Remember that when Gauthier was browsing through some art galleries, he came across a painting he thought was a real Modigliani – and one of the experts the shop owner called in agreed with him. He may just have a real talent for this sort of thing.

"Also, according to what Randy just told us about the art scene in Paris, both Ricci and Gauthier would probably have seen a real Fang Ngil mask in a museum somewhere. I presume that the appraiser who was hired to appraise the African masks for Old Art never had the same chance."

"My God," Randy said. "When I asked Hazel to take a better photograph of the white mask, it never crossed my mind it might be the real thing. But now I think you may be right. What really bothers me is that even if you *are* right, whoever donated that mask can't exactly ask for it back."

"Why not?" Pete asked.

"Because the people who donate stuff to Old Art give up all rights to it. I've seen the contract they have to sign, and it's pretty comprehensive!" Randy said.

"Randy's right," Julian said. "And as far as I know, Old Art has no obligation to sell everything it gets from donors within a set period of time. And things do get lost and misplaced. If this is a real Fang Ngil mask, they've probably hidden it for a while. Since the donor clearly had no idea what he was donating, they could just tell him they had sold all the colorfully painted masks as a case lot, but they were waiting to get some more white masks so that they could sell the white one in a case lot, too."

Jupiter was impressed with this hypothesis and also struck by how complicated this case might become. For a time he'd imagined that the directors of Old Art might be embezzling money from their company, but as of now, it was pretty clear that their scheme involved stealing certain valuable donations instead of sending them to auction.

Since the donors were anonymous and got the same tax breaks whatever the items they'd donated might make − or *not* make − it might actually be pretty easy to remove valuable items from their warehouse from time to time.

What Randy and Julian had said about the interns having to do their own estimates for the auction catalogues actually made a lot more sense all of a sudden. It might have been easy to simply black out the names of the donors, in order to keep them anonymous, but it wouldn't be so easy to black out certain items −

or their values!

While the others continued to talk about these issues, Jupiter had a sudden impulse to go outside and clear his head. If only he could remember whatever it was he couldn't remember, it might set the whole investigation on a better track. He stood up and excused himself, saying he'd be back in ten or fifteen minutes.

Once outside, Jupiter took deep breaths, then stood indecisively, wondering whether to go to HQ1. As he stood looking around him, he saw Leif Haldorsson walking from his workshop to the shed where the lumber was stored. Leif waved to him and he waved back. He strolled over to join him, and when he had, Jupiter launched into the sort of small talk he rarely, if ever, engaged in, except when he was acting.

"So how's it going? Are you working on something special today?" he asked Leif.

"Not really," Leif said. "Magnus and I are just finishing up the Scandinavian sideboard we've been making for our parents' 30th anniversary."

"You still need wood for that?" Jupiter asked.

"Not for that, no," Leif said. "Your aunt just heard from a customer who wants to buy another block of the wood she sold him four or five days ago. I'm checking to make sure we have some."

"What kind of wood is he looking for?" Jupiter asked, though he wasn't all that interested in the answer.

"It's an African wood called pearwood," Leif said, as he poked around a pile in the corner of the lumber shed. "It has a fine texture and a straight grain. The tree can grow two hundred feet high, with no branches for the first hundred feet. That's a lot of trunk to turn into smooth lumber without any knots."

"Really?" Jupiter said.

"I'd never used it before," Leif said, "but a client wanted a small table made of it. It's got a lot of silica in it, which gives it an odd shimmer. I didn't like the way it dulled my blades. I probably won't use it again, even though I have a bunch left over. But the man was delighted."

He bent over and grabbed a block in triumph. "And he's going to be delighted again!" he said.

As Jupiter looked at the block of wood, it suddenly struck him that the man Leif was referring to was the man he and the others had met the other day. He'd been wearing a black dashiki with a colorful yoke, and a bright kente hat.

"Is he the man from Ghana?" Jupiter asked intently.

"Yes, he is," Leif said, surprised. "He told me that in Ghana he was part of an artisans' workshop that made modern pieces based on traditional African art for international vendors. Museum shops and catalogues — that sort of thing. He said he was using the pearwood to make some sort of African mask."

"He actually said that?" Jupiter asked.

"Yes," Leif said. "He also asked about your new Headquarters, and I told him your names and what you did. He said he had two children, a boy and a girl, and that he and his family were all hoping to become American citizens soon. I liked him," Leif added.

"And he's coming to get another piece today?"

"He's on his way right now," Leif said. "He's got a lot of energy — he's a real entrepreneur — and he told me he was trying to set up his own business. He's selling his stuff on Amazon and Etsy and eBay at the moment, but he has big plans — and a big commission at the moment."

Jupiter felt a kind of warmth rush through him. His ears almost tingled.

"Do you remember anything else he said?" Jupiter asked.

"The commission is from another artist," Leif responded. 'He said the guy was very talented and did the same sort of thing he did."

"By which he meant?" Jupiter asked.

"He said the guy does excellent reproductions of drawings and paintings – at least judging from what was hanging on his walls."

"On the walls of his house?" Jupiter asked.

"I have no idea," Leif said. "He told me he was impressed that what the guy did was sort of what he'd learned to do back in Africa." By now, Leif was walking back toward his workshop, with Jupiter right beside him. "I had the impression he meant learning about other people's art."

"Thanks a lot," Jupiter said. "I've got to go!"

He turned on his heel and almost ran back to HQ2 – though he stopped before he got there to think out what he was going to say. The minute he remembered his meeting with Kwame Owusu, the whole thing had come together in his mind. But even now that Leif had given him exactly the sort of information that would confirm it, he couldn't decide how best to start explaining to the others what he thought Old Art was actually up to.

As he stood thinking, a truck drove into the Salvage Yard and Kwame Owusu himself got out. He wore the same kente hat but a different dashiki. He looked very regal but he didn't seem as upbeat and happy as he had the other day when he'd met The Three Investigators as he was leaving the Salvage Yard. He seemed deep in thought, but when he saw Jupiter, he broke into a smile.

"Hello, Jupiter Jones," he said.

"Hello, Mr. Owusu," Jupiter replied. "Leif has your pearwood waiting for you in his workshop, but I wonder if you could answer a question first."

"I can try," Mr. Owusu said.

"As you know, my friends and I are investigators," Jupiter said, "and right now we're investigating a local nonprofit foundation called Old Art For Young Artists. Do you know anything about them, by any chance?"

Kwame Owusu looked astounded.

"I did not until ten days ago," he said. "Then I got an e-mail from a man named Giovanni Ricci. He had found my Facebook page and saw that when I worked in Africa, the International Artists Network had sponsored the workshop I worked for."

"Did he ask you to make a reproduction of a Fang Ngil mask for him?" asked Jupiter.

At this, Kwame Owusu looked even more astounded.

"Yes, he did," he said. "When I wrote back to him, he invited me to his house. On his table were eight photographs – very high quality, of a Fang Ngil mask."

"So he gave you the photographs to work from?" Jupiter asked.

Mr. Owusu nodded. "Yes. But first he asked me if I was sure I could do the work. I told him I could. It had to be done quickly, he said. And I had to buy my own materials. He offered to pay me $4000, which is very big money. He gave me half then and told me he would give me the rest when I brought him the mask. I liked him and I liked his work."

He stopped and looked at Jupiter. "But how did you know?" he asked.

"It's a pretty long story," Jupiter said. "Do you have time to come into our Headquarters and talk to us about it? My friends are there. So is a guy who worked for Old Art as an intern last summer, and another guy who's working for them right now."

Mr. Owusu looked alarmed.

"What I am doing is quite legitimate, I assure you. I am almost finished with the mask, and I am very happy with it. I do not like to boast, but I think it is very good. I think it is so good that I came to buy more pearwood. I will make another one – not for Mr. Ricci, but to sell through my Facebook page."

"I'm sorry to tell you this, Mr. Owusu," Jupiter said, "but although you're doing nothing wrong, my friends and I have reason to believe that Giovanni Ricci and his partners may be doing something illegal with your mask."

"Do you mean they are not honest?" Mr. Owusu said.

Jupiter nodded. "I'm afraid they may not be honest," he said.

"But... but ...," Mr. Owusu sputtered. "I did not know!"

Jupiter could see he was clearly very upset by the suggestion that he'd been involved in something illegal.

"Of course you didn't," Jupiter said. "And no matter what happens, you won't be in any trouble. But you could help us out a lot if you'd be willing to talk with us."

"I see," said Mr. Owusu. "Well, in that case, I will."

"Great," Jupiter said. "Just wait a minute while I tell the others you're coming. Or better yet, go get your pearwood from Leif, then come to Headquarters when you're finished."

"I will do that," Mr. Owusu said.

Jupiter dashed into Headquarters. Pete was opening sodas, Bob was plating up turkey and tomato sandwiches, and the other four were sitting around the enormous table in the little kitchenette.

"We're going to have to put lunch off," he said, as everyone looked at him in surprise. "The key to the whole investigation has just driven into the Salvage Yard. Mr. Kwame Owusu, originally from Ghana."

To Randy and Julian, he said, "We met him a few days ago when he came to buy some special wood, and it turns out he's working for Giovanni Ricci. Making a reproduction Fang Ngil mask. I haven't seen the photographs he's working from, but I'll bet they're a whole lot better than the ones Randy's friend Hazel took in the warehouse."

"You mean that after they removed the Fang Ngil mask from the warehouse, they hired Kwame Owusu to copy it?" Julian asked.

"That's right," Jupiter said. "And he's gotten the job done already. He came back to get more pearwood, to make a second mask."

"Oh, no," Randy said. "That wouldn't be smart. If the crooks at Old Art were to get wind of the fact that this guy was making a second copy of a mask that was supposed to be one of a kind, they'd be pissed, to put it mildly."

"That's exactly what I thought," Jupiter said. "Although I was impressed with Randy's hypothesis that Old Art might be planning to tell the donor that the missing mask had gotten lost or misplaced or had been separated out from the other masks, it now seems they thought it would be safer if they had a high-quality reproduction made. They clearly plan to sell *that* at the auction – and then to sell the original to a private buyer when they think it's safe. The thing is..."

"Oh, no!" Bob said. "At the Gala, Mallory and I heard Gauthier and his wife discussing someone who they said would never guess what Old Art was up to in a million years, but if he did, he might be their biggest danger."

"That's right," Mallory said. "They said the man was naive – but a lot cleverer than you might think from hearing his accent. That *has* to be Kwame Owusu!"

"I agree," said Jupiter. "And if they were

already worried about whether they could trust him, they'd be *really* worried if they thought he was going to put a duplicate of the mask up for sale on his Facebook page."

"But they wouldn't really *do* anything to him, would they?" Randy asked. "I mean, they may be crooks, but they aren't murderers!"

"I wouldn't be too sure of that," Jupiter said.

"I wouldn't either," said Mallory. "At the Gala, Juanita Guadalupe said that aside from his family, Kwame Owusu didn't know anyone in this country, and if he was the victim of a hit and run, no one would care too much."

"A hit and run?" Randy said. "I wonder why she said *that*."

"Whatever you do, don't scare Kwame Owusu by telling him that part of the story!" Jupiter said.

Just then, there was a knock on the front door of HQ2, and when Pete went to open it, a worried-looking Kwame Owusu stood in the doorway.

11

An Ingenious Con

As Pete stood back to let Kwame Owusu in, he fervently hoped the man hadn't overheard the last part of the conversation. Eavesdropping was all very well − and very useful − when you intended to do it, Pete reflected, but when it was accidental, it could be quite upsetting to the hearer.

"Come in," he said. "Great to see you. Can I get you a soda or a sandwich?"

"Most kind," Mr. Owusu said, "but no, thank you. I am eager to tell Jupiter and the other Investigators what I know." Looking beyond Pete, he suddenly saw the set table.

"But you are eating," he said. "Perhaps this is not a good time."

"It's a fine time," Jupiter said firmly. "Our lunch can wait. This is Julian Jackson, who worked for Old Art For Young Artists last summer, and this is Randy Foreman, who's working for them now."

"Ah," Mr. Owusu said, stepping forward. When Pete saw the respectful confidence with which he shook Randy and Julian's hands,

193

then arranged his dashiki around him as he took a seat on the sofa, Pete was suddenly convinced that, with his help, they were going to get to the bottom of whatever was going on at Old Art For Young Artists.

In a way, he was glad of that, but in another way he wasn't. He'd been thinking about what his father had told him about Alyssa Ricci – what a lovely woman she was, and how she'd been in love with Giovanni ever since the two of them were high school sweethearts.

Although he knew it was silly, when he'd heard that, he'd thought of himself and Califia – how, in a way, they were also high school sweethearts. Well, not in a way, but really. And although the two of them had been dating for less than a year now, and most of the people who knew them assumed that all they had was a high school romance, Pete wasn't so sure. Although he and Califia were very different in a lot of ways, they both preferred the real world to the online one, and they almost always had fun together.

Also, in recent weeks, they'd started talking more seriously about their hopes and plans for the future, and when Pete had been late to the Three Investigators' meeting the day before the Gala, it wasn't just because Califia had been telling him the plot of *West Side Story*. She'd been talking about her role in it, and how it required a whole different set of skills than she'd used in other plays, and how skills had to be practiced. Though you might have been born with a bigger talent than someone else, you weren't born knowing how to use it, she'd said.

Pete had thought that was really smart of her, and he'd told her sports were like that, too. Ever since he could remember, he'd been better at ball games than the average boy, but he would never have made the varsity baseball and soccer teams if he hadn't practiced, practiced, and then practiced some more, the whole time he was growing up.

Pete had also told Califia that one of the things he loved about being a member of The Three Investigators was that they had never encountered a single mystery that hadn't taught him something new and interesting. It was great to be able to talk to her about things that mattered to him – and already he was hoping he might be talking to her that way for a long time to come.

That was why he was feeling sympathy for Alyssa Ricci at the thought that her husband's foundation was a blind for criminal activity. It was a pity when innocent people got caught up in things like this. But after all, Mr. Owusu was innocent, too − and although he *didn't* seem to have overheard the remarks about drastic action and doing away with someone, he seemed worried, anyway.

"From what Jupiter told me, I am wishing that I'd never answered Giovanni Ricci's e-mail!" he said.

"I can understand that," Jupiter said. "But you could help us a lot if you'd be willing to tell us what you know. To start, you said that on Facebook you say that, among other things, you make reproductions of traditional African masks, and about ten days ago you got an e-mail asking if you could make a specific mask on commission from photographs."

"Yes," Mr. Owusu said. "That is correct."

"You then went to the house of Mr. Giovanni Ricci who showed you photographs of the mask he wanted you to copy?"

"A Fang Ngil mask," Mr. Owusu said. "I told him I could do it, and he offered me the money. I am supposed to take it to his house either tomorrow or the day after tomorrow at 8:00 at night."

"You said you liked him, and that you

also liked his work. What kind of artist is he?"

"A painter," Mr. Owusu said. "He has a studio in his house, and I could smell the turpentine and linseed oil and oil paint in the air. And there were paintings on his wall, very good. All reproductions, or imitations – very different from one another."

"How did you know they were not originals?" Jupiter said.

"People who live in modest houses do not have Picassos on the wall," Mr. Owusu said. "My teacher in Ghana taught me quite a lot about art, and if the paintings on Mr. Ricci's wall were not copies, they would be in museums. He had Chagall, Mondrian, Modigliani. All modern painters."

"Modigliani!" Mallory said.

"It looked exactly like a Modigliani," Mr. Owusu said, "though I had seen it before, in a book. A portrait of a boy, with the very long neck and face. I asked Mr. Ricci if he had done it, and he said yes. I told him how wonderful it was. He was very pleased."

"Did you mention Modigliani?" Jupiter asked. "Did you say you knew it was a copy?"

"Oh, no," Mr. Owusu said. "That would have been very impolite. My teacher told me never to talk about whether something was a copy unless you were the person who made it. Very bad manners."

"So is it possible," Jupiter asked, "that he believed you thought it was an original?"

"Yes," Mr. Owusu said. "That is why I complimented him."

The more Mr. Owusu talked, the more Pete liked him. He clearly was someone who wanted to think the best of everyone, and who was honest and aboveboard in all his dealings. He hoped Jupiter would return the courtesy.

And to Pete's pleasure, Jupiter did.

"Mr. Owusu," Jupiter said. "I know we can trust you with what I'm about to say. We have been sure for several days that Mr. Ricci and his partners were up to something. When we started the investigation, I thought they were embezzling money from the foundation they themselves set up. But now I believe they've been laundering art works, so to speak."

"I do not understand," Mr. Owusu said.

"They accept donations of art, which they auction off to make money for their foundation. I think they're switching forged copies for some of the donated ones, and auctioning them as though they're the ones that were donated. They profit twice. Proceeds from the forgery go to the foundation. Then they sell the original secretly."

Not only Mr. Owusu, but Pete and everyone else in Headquarters was staring at Jupiter in amazement.

Randy Foreman quickly recovered. "We knew that Ricci was an artist," he said. "But from what Mr. Owusu has told us he may be far more talented than we had any reason to suppose."

Julian nodded in something like awe. "So talented, in fact, that he's capable of painting copies that survive close scrutiny!"

"That's right," Jupiter said. "If the appraisal of a particular painting was high, they'd remove it from the warehouse for a few days and take detailed photographs. Then Ricci would copy it and Old Art would auction off Ricci's forgery. The person who bought it would be highly unlikely to question the appraisal of a foundation that supposedly helps the disadvantaged. Then Old Art could sell the original painting on the private market somewhere."

Mallory nodded. "I'm suddenly thinking about that article I read about Rémy Gauthier browsing through shops and galleries on the Left Bank and coming across a painting that he told the shopkeeper was probably by Modigliani," she said.

"I don't remember hearing about that," Pete said.

"You weren't there that day," Bob said. "It was the afternoon of the Gala, when you were working at the Rescue Center. Gauthier told the shop owner that he thought the painting was original – and one of the experts the shop owner called in agreed!"

"But you think it had really been painted by Ricci?" Pete asked.

"Now that we know what we know, it seems likely," said Mallory. "And if it's true, then Ricci really is extraordinarily talented."

"Extraordinarily talented," Julian said, "and extraordinarily crafty as well. After all, a good art forger has to make sure that the paint and canvas and frame he uses can all be seen as authentic and more or less like they fit with the original date of the painting. And he has to master the technique used by the artist. He can't just copy a painting."

"That's true," said Mallory. "But to me, the really interesting thing about the story is that neither Ricci nor Gauthier made a penny off the sale of that painting – though identifying it led to Gauthier getting a job offer in the United States."

"It did?" Julian asked.

"That's what the article I found suggested," Mallory said. "But if Ricci actually painted it − then got it planted in that gallery − the only thing *he* got out of it was the pleasure of having an expert think he'd painted an actual Modigliani!"

"And the far more dubious pleasure of having Rémy Gauthier suggest they go into business together," said Jupiter.

"Wow," Pete said. "Did someone buy that Paris painting?"

"You bet," said Mallory. "A private collector who really loved the piece and bought it for a lot of money. He said he chose to believe it *was* a Modigliani! Clearly it wouldn't be a problem for Ricci to copy just about anything well enough to convince a buyer at a public auction."

"That sounds right," Randy said. "But in the case of the Fang Ngil mask, which was worth so much, they had to find another artist who could copy it. That was where Mr. Owusu came in."

"Holy smoke," Julian said. "I'm totally blown away."

"Yes," Jupiter said. "It's an ingenious con. Right from the start we thought it was odd that Old Art only hired young people as interns – and then only for three months. It seems they only hired interns who wouldn't know anything solid about the kind of art that Giovanni Ricci can forge. They couldn't let anyone near the warehouse who might notice something suspicious when the paintings were switched."

"So they only ran the scam with paintings," Mallory said.

"Or drawings," Jupiter said. "Apparently those are the two areas of Ricci's expertise. Anything else that was donated – rugs, or Chinese vases, or antique metalworking, or sculpture, or things made of wood or gold – were simply put up for auction, more or less honestly."

"Honest, except for that guy who bid up the prices," Pete reminded him.

"Yes," Jupiter said, smiling grimly. "In fact, probably nothing other than paintings or drawings has ever tempted them before. If they switched only fine art that Ricci could forge, they had no need to find anyone else to collaborate with them. Then someone or other donated the masks. Quite obviously whoever it was had no idea that one of the masks was worth a fortune. But either Ricci or Gauthier

202

or both of them knew what they had."

Kwame Owusu nodded. "I begin to understand," he said.

"We think that when they were in Paris, they may have studied Fang Ngil masks," Jupiter continued. "And when they saw what had come into their warehouse, it was just too good an opportunity to pass up. I expect that almost nothing would have tempted them to involve someone outside the three of them. Except this. I don't know whether the appraiser was crooked, or just ignorant, but he listed the mask as a reproduction – which was exactly what they'd be auctioning off! That's where Mr. Owusu came in."

Mr. Owusu nodded solemnly.

"I wonder what they'd have done if they were honest," Pete said. "When they found out what their donor had really given them."

"They should have felt morally compelled to tell him, or her, that they believed the appraisal was incorrect," Jupiter said.

"You can say that again," Pete said. "Like it was only off by $4,950,000 or something!"

As Pete spoke, he didn't know whether to be appalled or flooded with admiration at the audacity of Old Art's scam. Many of the criminals the Three Investigators had caught had used blunt force or blunt ideas. Slade De-Marco had just bashed his way around in the world, and even the ICE agent and his Greek partner hadn't been too subtle in their plan or approach. But Gauthier, Guadalupe, and Ricci had taken their sweet time to set up this scam. It had layers to it, and it was subtle.

If only people like them turned their talents and their brains to doing good instead of thinking up elaborate ways to enrich themselves, the world would be a better place, Pete thought. They'd established a nonprofit – ha, ha! very funny – with the supposed aim of funneling money to young artists when their real aim was funneling money to themselves. Giovanni Ricci painted copies of paintings that had been donated; then they auctioned off the copies and sold the originals under the table. It was clever, but also illegal and wicked – especially because they were using the current divide-and-conquer politics of America as a cover.

He hoped Mr. Owusu wasn't too freaked out by what he'd just learned, because from the peculiar gleam in Jupiter's eye, Pete was sure that Jupiter was hoping to involve him in a plan that even now was taking shape in the back of

Jupiter's brain. He didn't know what it was. Would he want Mr. Owusu to carry a small tape recorder? Or talk to the police? He thought it would likely be some sort of sting.

"So what are they going to do with the mask?" Pete asked.

"I'm sure by now they have a network of shady connections," Jupiter said. "They could never take the risk of letting any of the works Ricci copied be auctioned off by a fine arts auctioneer. Far too much publicity. Besides, the person who donated the item would have been certain to find out. They probably have a fence who can put the mask in the hands of an unscrupulous foreign collector. I'm sure they wanted to get all the art they stole out of the country."

"So how are we going to get them?" Pete asked. "Have you worked out a plan yet?"

Jupiter looked out the French doors toward the outdoor workshop and shook his head.

"Not really," he said. "Though I'm still hopeful that the application I filled out this morning will have a set of clean fingerprints Chief Reynolds's men can dust."

Since Julian, Randy, and Kwame Owusu didn't know what he was talking about, he explained, then added, "I made a call to the station earlier this morning. Chief Reynolds isn't there today, but we have an appointment to see him tomorrow."

"Great!" said Pete.

"I'd also like to go see Peggy Thomas – a woman who recently made a donation to Old Art For Young Artists. We met her at the Gala the other night. She might be able to give us some insights into the donation process."

Pete noticed that Julian Jackson was looking at Jupiter strangely. "Peggy Thomas?" he said. "I know a Peggy Thomas. Or rather, Uncle Cornelius does."

"A dancer who was married to a jazz musician?" Jupiter asked.

"That's right!" Julian said. "He played in Harlem, and she danced in New York before they moved out to California. How wild that you met her at the Gala! Lyle and Uncle Cornelius and I never saw her there! You knew that her husband Clay had recently died?"

"Yes, she told us that," Pete said. "She was there with my girlfriend's parents."

"Who's your girlfriend?" asked Julian.

"Her name is Califia García-Williams," Pete said. "Her father's an actor, and her mother's a dancer."

"I don't think I've met her," Julian said thoughtfully. "But I *have* met Peggy Thomas. You say she told you she recently donated something to Old Art? Did she say what it was?"

"No," Jupiter said. "And I wasn't smart enough to ask her. That's why I'd like to talk to her again."

"Could we come with you?" Julian said. "We could drive you in Randy's car. I've gotten quite fond of roaring around Los Angeles looking like a surfer!"

"It's a plan," Jupiter said. "Or part of a plan, at least. But in addition to meeting with Peggy Thomas and Chief Reynolds, I've been thinking that maybe we should meet with Alyssa and Giovanni Ricci. When Mallory and Bob were surveilling Old Art at the Gala, they saw the two of them together and thought they looked like they really loved each other. They also had the strong impression that Alyssa wasn't part of the con and that she didn't know what was really going on."

"That's right," Mallory said. "And Guadalupe and Gauthier said that Ricci wanted to leave the foundation as soon as the baby was born." She turned to Kwame Owusu and added, "She's having a baby soon."

"Babies are great blessings," Mr. Owusu said.

"So here's what I propose," Jupiter said, "though it depends on Mr. Owusu's permission."

Here we go, Pete thought. I knew Jupiter had an idea!

"When Mr. Owusu delivers the mask he's made to Giovanni Ricci's house," Jupiter said, "the four of us go with him."

Mr. Owusu looked quite startled. "Why would I take you with me?" he asked.

"Because we're working for you this summer as your interns," Jupiter said.

"My interns?" Mr. Owusu said. "But I am a one-man operation."

"That may be so," Jupiter said, "but what if you're teaching us how to set up a small business? How to use the Internet to sell things? And how to work as an independent contractor?"

Mr. Owusu didn't look like the sort of person who would have interns, Pete thought, but he was interested in how the man would react.

"I think Giovanni Ricci will be so surprised that he won't ask too many questions," Jupiter continued. "And because his wife will be

there – we can only hope! – he'll feel quite con-
strained in what he says and does. We'll use
any opportunities we're given to ask questions
or get further leads or information. If nothing
comes of it, then all we've wasted is an hour or
two. And if Ricci is as good an artist as Mr.
Owusu says, he may have a moral center that
the other two lack."

"Yes, indeed," Mr. Owusu said. "I think
he is very good. It is too bad he is not doing his
own work but is using his talent, which is given
to him by God, to cheat other people."

He sat back on the sofa, his hands
clasped before him, trying to compose his face
and his thoughts. "I do not like to fool
anyone," he said, "even a bad person, so I do
not know how I feel about your idea, Jupiter."

He sat up straighter. "But I also do not
like to be played for the fool," he said. "I do
not like to be used. And if Mr. Ricci has asked
me to produce a copy of a true Fang Ngil
mask and then plans to sell that mask to a private collector, then they are involving me in
stealing the mask from their own organization."

"Yes," Jupiter said. "I think that's true."

"So," Mr. Owusu said. "It would be
wrong of me not to help catch these people.

And you say that they are setting people against other people by race? Why, that is wicked all by itself! That is exactly what America is supposed to stand against!"

Pete could see that though Kwame Owusu was usually a happy and peaceable man, he was now quite irate. He stood and re-arranged his cap on his head. As he did, he seemed to compose himself as well. He smiled and nodded at each of them in turn. "I am glad to have met you both," he said to Julian and Randy, "though I wish that everything was happier. How should I get in touch with you?" he said to Jupiter.

Jupiter took out his wallet and gave Mr. Owusu a Three Investigators card.

"Ah," he said as he examined it. "Someone is an artist!"

"That's our friend Connor O'Malley!" Pete said enthusiastically. "He designed the chimera."

"Is that what you call it?" Mr. Owusu said. "It is a most fearsome beast."

"I'm the bighorn sheep," Pete said. "Bob's the bobcat, and Jupiter's the eagle."

Mr. Owusu nodded sagely. "I am very glad to know that. Thank you for this. I will call you as soon as I learn when I am to take the mask to Mr. Ricci."

"That will be great," Jupiter said. "Thanks for helping us."

Mr. Owusu bowed from the waist, just a little. "I will look forward to seeing you all again," he said, and then he was gone.

Pete stared at his friends for a moment, then looked at the sandwiches still sitting on the table. In the end, he and Julian made a dash for them, while the others followed a little bit more slowly.

Pete was still eating when Bob suddenly said, "Oh, no. I just remembered about my father's article and Guadalupe and Gauthier figuring out I was the son of the guy who had interviewed him. I'm going to have to tell Dad about it when I get home tonight – and I'm not looking forward to it at all!"

12

A Machiavellian Man

As Bob biked home, he kept thinking about what to say to his father. How to bring the topic up? How to explain? But when he arrived, his father wasn't there. As his mother made dinner, she told Bob that his father's editor had called him in for an unusual Sunday night meeting at the central office in Los Angeles.

"That's weird," Bob said. A small knot was forming in his stomach.

"He said he'd be getting home pretty late," Bob's mother said. As Bob helped her clean up the kitchen after dinner, he realized he'd been tense, subdued, and out of sorts ever since he'd lost his cool at the Jobs Fair. In fact, even now, he was still annoyed at himself for leaving his application and for letting Guadalupe see how upset he'd been.

He hadn't exactly divulged information, but in a way he had. He'd acted peculiarly, which had drawn her attention to him. He was probably the only person in the history of the world who had gotten upset when someone offered him seventy-five dollars.

There had to have been a more graceful way for him to turn down the grant and get out of there, but he'd just bolted, leaving his paperwork behind. He felt like a complete idiot, especially since the others had all remembered to take theirs, and Jupiter had even managed to make off with the woman's fingerprints!

He would have thought that, by this time, he wouldn't be brooding so much about the morning. He was, though – and oddly enough, he was also brooding about the way Pete had talked about Califia in response to Julian asking how they knew Peggy Thomas.

All he'd done was call Califia his girlfriend – but he'd done it with such confidence and happiness that it had made Bob envious. Not *really* envious. That would be stupid – especially because Pete himself had just recently urged him to go for it with Leif and Magnus Haldorsson's sister, Freya.

Still, the more Bob thought about it, the more he wished he would bump into Freya one of these days. Or not just bump into her. Have the chance to take her on a date. Until he did, there was no chance at all that he'd ever have her as his girlfriend, or even know if that was what he wanted. When he had first met her, he'd thought she was pretty young, and maybe even a bit shallow, but she'd grown up a lot since then.

In fact, the few times he'd seen her over the last year – when she'd come to the Salvage Yard with Leif or Magnus – she'd seemed pretty mature. She'd sort of settled into herself, he thought.

A little while later, Bob was sitting at the desk in his bedroom, idly surfing around the Internet, when his cell phone rang. He was surprised to see it was his father.

"Dad!" he said.

"Bob?" his father said, his voice shaky with anger.

Bob's father sounded so riled up that Bob knew at once what must have happened. He wanted to say, "I know what you're upset about, and I can explain," but no words came out.

His father's voice was very tense. "Were you at a jobs fair at the city park earlier?" his father asked. "Did you apply for a mini-grant from an organization called Old Art for Young Artists?"

Bob was flooded with dread – and for some strange reason he couldn't bring himself to simply answer his father in a straightforward way.

"Pete, Mallory, Jupe, and I were on a case," he said. "How did you know?"

"I just got out of a meeting with Larry Winthrop at the *Sun*. He told me he'd gotten a very heated call from a man named Rémy Gauthier earlier today. Mr. Gauthier thinks I asked you – my famous Three Investigators son! – to go undercover, by applying for a grant you don't need from an organization I was writing an article on. I told you the other morning that I was writing a feature piece about Old Art," Bob's father said.

"No, you didn't," Bob said. "You never told me the name of the nonprofit, or of the man you were going off to interview. I didn't know until after it all happened that we were investigating the very same foundation you're supposed to be writing about."

Just a half hour earlier, Bob had been feeling like a complete idiot for getting so upset at the interview, but this conversation with his father somehow allowed him to feel – quite rightly – that he'd done nothing wrong.

Bob's speech took some of the fire out of his father's voice. "That's all I said to you about it? That I was writing about a local nonprofit?"

"That's all," Bob said.

"O.K., then," his father said, considerably calmer. "My mistake. I guess you're right. Sorry for going off on you like that. But even so, I wish you'd mentioned what you and your friends were up to, because I'm now in a very awkward position."

It sounded to Bob as if it had been a bad day for the Andrews men. "What exactly happened?" Bob asked.

"According to Winthrop – who got this from Gauthier, of course – you were very rude to the woman who interviewed you, and that when she offered you a grant, you shoved the money back at her, got up, and stormed off. You must have had a very good reason, because your mother and I didn't bring you up to behave like that."

"I know," Bob said.

"Anyway, Winthrop's taken me off the story. Although I normally wouldn't be too bothered, in this case I'm working fewer days a week because of my book, and the article was freelance, and I really don't want to lose the money."

"I'm sorry, Dad," Bob said. He felt awful.

"Oh, well," Mr. Andrews said. "It wasn't your fault. You didn't know."

"But in a way it *was* my fault," Bob said. "I never should have acted the way I did. And I stupidly left my name and contact information on the application. I was supposed to take it away with me, but I got so angry I forgot."

"Most people don't get angry when they're offered $75," his father said.

"Well, I did," Bob said. "I think Old Art for New Artists is up to exactly what you wrote about in that chapter of your book that caused such a ruckus."

"What do you mean?" his father asked.

"The only reason Ms. Guadalupe offered me the grant is because I'm part Asian," Bob said. "She turned down Mallory, who needs the grant much more than I do."

"Really?" his father said. "That's very interesting. So you think Gauthier and his partners are using tribal politics to advance a hidden agenda? Or maybe not so hidden, if The Three Investigators are onto it. Maybe I can do a bit of real investigative journalism again – with the help of my famous son!"

Here were two reasons Bob loved his father so much – he never stayed angry long, and he was almost as quick as Jupiter to put two and two together and get a solid four.

"As I told you the other morning, the

truth is that even before that chapter was published, and my boss was bombarded with e-
mails and texts and tweets, he had already
been getting nervous about my writing. It's as
if he doesn't want to publish anything that
might ruffle anyone's feathers. He wants puff
pieces – and if I had written one in this case, it
sounds as if I might have been writing a puff
piece about a Machiavellian villain!"

Although Bob had heard the word Machiavellian from time to time, he didn't know
exactly what it meant and was glad when his
father explained.

"Machiavelli was an Italian philosopher
who wrote a book about the uses of deception,
treachery, and crime – and from what you've
just told me about Old Art's *modus operandi*,
someone in that foundation has studied at the
feet of the master! Listen, I'm hanging up and
driving home now. Go to bed if you want to.
We can talk about this some other time."

After a good night's sleep, Bob felt better, and after breakfast he enjoyed his morning
bike ride to the Salvage Yard. The Albertson
children were bouncing on the trampoline
again. They looked as if they were reaching for
the stars, and as he watched them, Bob
couldn't help but think that to teach young chil-

dren like the Albertsons that they were somehow "oppressors" because of their skin color was really twisted. If they believed the lie, they would never bounce as high again.

At the Salvage Yard, Bob learned that Julian Jackson had made an appointment with Peggy Thomas for early that afternoon. After The Three Investigators got back from their meeting with Chief Reynolds, Julian and Randy would be coming by to take them to her house.

They locked their bikes in a bike rack in front of the police station, unbuckled their helmets, and carried them in. There seemed to be a lot going on at the station this morning, and it took a while for the Chief to be ready to see them.

While they sat together in a corner of the waiting room, Bob filled the others in on his conversation with his father.

"And then he said that if he was fired, at least he'd have more time to write the stuff he wants to write, instead of what he called puff pieces about Machiavellian villains," Bob told them. "I thought that was cool. Although I'm not actually all that familiar with Machiavelli, at least I know his name begins with an M! Just like mask!"

Bob hadn't thought that Jupiter had

been listening all that hard to what he was saying, but it turned out he was wrong.

"This spring I read a book about what is
called in psychology the "dark triad," Jupiter
said, "and Machiavellianism is one of the three.
They're called 'dark' because of their malevolent qualities, and almost all criminals have
some aspects of all three in their personalities."

"Whew!" said Pete. "That sounds pretty
scary!"

"It's meant to," Jupiter said. "The other
two traits are narcissism and psychopathy – but
Machiavellianism is the easiest to understand,
and also the one we've seen in a lot of our
cases. Machiavellian people are manipulative,
callous, and immoral. They're very deceitful,
and very low on empathy."

While Bob was rarely surprised by the
depth and breadth of Jupiter's knowledge, he
was surprised that Jupiter had read a book
about the criminal mind without having mentioned it to The Three Investigators. But when
he asked, Jupiter said it was a short book, and
that he'd read it over a single weekend.

He also said that he thought that, for the
time being, they should tell Chief Reynolds as
little as possible about what was going on with
Old Art For Young Artists – that they should

just explain what had happened at the Jobs Fair, linked with the suspicions of Sibyl Saskatchewan.

Just then, Chief Reynolds appeared in the doorway.

"You guys are growing up!" he said. "All I need to do is let you out of my sight and you sprout another six inches."

Pete laughed at the exaggeration. "You look exactly the same," he said.

"Well, at my age, that's a compliment," the chief said. "Let's go to my office so you can tell me all about the case."

However, once the four of them actually settled around his desk, Bob saw that Jupiter had been serious in not wanting to tell Chief Reynolds all about the case.

He mentioned nothing about the almost-certainly-authentic Fang Ngil mask, or what Julian Jackson and Randy Foreman had said about it, or the reproduction mask Kwame Owusu was making, or the plan to go to the Riccis' house the night Kwame delivered it to Giovanni, or even what Bob's father had suggested about Rémy Gauthier.

In fact, all Jupiter told the Chief was that he and his friends were investigating a non-profit foundation called Old Art For Young

Artists, because the woman who ran the Rocky Beach Costume Bank had told them she thought they were giving their grants almost solely to minorities, whether those minorities needed the grants or not. He also told him that when he and Pete had applied for jobs as interns, Pete had been offered one, while he hadn't, and when Mallory and Bob applied for mini-grants, Bob had been offered one and Mallory hadn't.

"Hmmm," said Chief Reynolds. "That suggests that the woman who runs the Costume Bank may have been onto something. What's her name, by the way?"

"Sibyl Saskatchewan," Jupiter said.

Chief Reynolds opened his eyes wide, threw his head back, and roared with laughter. When Bob and the others looked at him inquiringly, he explained, still laughing a little.

"I think I've run into her," he said. "I can't imagine there are two women with that name living in Rocky Beach, and if it's the same woman, I caught her skinny dipping in the pool at the City Park about thirty years ago. At night, when the pool was closed.

"I wasn't chief then, of course, just a rookie cop who'd been on the force about a month. When my partner got a call saying that someone had broken though the fence around the pool, we went roaring down to the Park – where we found one totally naked woman doing the backstroke! Needless to say, we didn't arrest her – though she did tell us her name. I guess it's stuck in my mind all these years because I was so embarrassed."

Bob had always liked Chief Reynolds, but he liked him even more after hearing this story. It was great when grown-ups like his father and Chief Reynolds trusted kids enough to be honest with them about their feelings and experiences.

Still, even after Chief Reynolds had been so frank, Jupiter still seemed determined to play things close to the chest. After smiling thinly at the Chief's story, he said, "The reason we're here isn't because of what Sibyl Saskatchewan told us, but because when I was being interviewed by Juanita Guadalupe, Rémy Gauthier's wife, I started to wonder if she had a criminal record. There's very little about her on the Internet. So I grabbed the application papers she'd handled, took them away with me, and put them in this manilla envelope." He held the envelope up. "I was hoping you could dust them for fingerprints, and if you found some, run them through your database."

"Hmm," Chief Reynolds said. "If you handled the papers, Jupiter, I'd have to take your fingerprints first, to make sure that whatever prints we run through the database aren't yours. And even then, we won't really be sure that whatever prints we *do* find are actually this woman's. Any number of other people might have handled application papers."

"I realize that," said Jupiter. "And we wouldn't be asking you to investigate Juanita Guadalupe or her partners. At least not now. Not until we had something solid. But if we knew she had a criminal record, we could proceed with extra caution."

This was the first time Bob had ever heard Jupiter suggest such a thing, and he smiled to himself at the thought. Chief Reynolds seemed entirely persuaded by the argument, though, and after he took the manilla envelope off to the lab at the back of the police station, he returned with an ink pad and some paper to take Jupiter's fingerprints.

As Chief Reynolds carefully rolled first Jupiter's thumb and then each separate finger, on each hand, across the ink pad and then onto the paper, Pete laughed.

"When Jupe applied for the internship with Old Art, I told him he should write on the application that his art form was printmaking. Because of when he made ink prints of his feet to make sure that his birth certificate was really his. But this is even better!" he said.

"At least if he turns out to be right about Juanita Guadalupe," said Chief Reynolds, smiling at the joke. He handed Jupiter a cloth to wipe his hands with before he gathered together the ink pad and papers and took them back to the lab. He was back in what seemed like no time – but just to say that it would take about half an hour for the lab to get the results, and that the four of them should go back to the waiting room while the tests were being run.

It seemed a long wait for the Chief this time, and although they talked a bit more while they were waiting, Jupiter seemed very tense. At last, Chief Reynolds appeared in the doorway and waved to them to come with him. When they were sitting again in the straight-backed chairs in his office, Chief Reynolds looked at Jupiter gravely.

"Your instincts are excellent, Jupiter," he said. "As always. My men found only one set of prints, other than yours, on the application papers, and when they ran the prints through the database, they discovered that Juanita

Guadalupe's original name was Anna Maldonado. She's a con artist with a rap sheet as long as her arm. She was born in Mexico, but grew up in Las Vegas where she ran various cons at casinos and churches. When things got hot in Nevada, she skipped across the border and changed her name."

"Legally?" Jupiter asked.

"Yes," the chief said. "She's now legally Juanita Guadalupe. That took some cheek, since Our Lady of Guadalupe is another name for the Virgin Mary. She's stayed clean since she got to California, apparently. Though it seems she and this Gauthier guy can barely have known each other when they got married."

"That's what we thought," Bob said. "That they got married for reasons having nothing to do with love. Either they did it so that Gauthier could stay in the country as long as he wanted, or so that the two of them would never be forced to testify against one another in court."

"It certainly looks that way," said the Chief. "But there's something else my men turned up about Juanita Guadalupe – something a bit more serious than a con. It's not on her rap sheet because it never went to trial or got pled out, but when she was still living in Las Vegas, she was arrested for a hit and run."

"A hit and run!" Pete cried. "But – !"

"But what?" Chief Reynolds asked, looking at him keenly.

"But nothing," Pete said, starting to blush. To Bob and Jupiter, this would have been a dead giveaway that he was concealing something, but either Chief Reynolds didn't notice the blush or he thought it would be impolite to comment on it.

"I mean, I thought hit and runs were a serious crime," Pete said.

"They are," said Chief Reynolds. "Especially when the person hit by the car actually dies. In this case, the man who died was Juanita Guadalupe's boss. Ex-boss, I should say. He'd fired her the day he was hit. There was a witness who claimed to have seen Juanita Guadalupe at the wheel of the car that struck him, but the police were never able to find any physical evidence. Still, if this had been *my* case, I would have retained the liveliest suspicions of this woman. I do hope the four of you will be careful!"

"We will," Jupiter said. "And if we get something solid on Juanita Guadalupe or Rémy Gauthier, we'll let you know what we've discovered."

But as Jupiter got to his feet and shook Chief Reynolds's hand, Bob had the strong impression that, even now, he wasn't being entirely honest with the Chief.

13

An Idea About How To Set the Situation Straight

Fifteen minutes later, as Jupiter wheeled his bike into the Salvage Yard, he knew that, as soon as they got to HQ2, he was going to have to explain to the others why he had been so close-mouthed with Chief Reynolds. The problem was, he really wasn't sure himself. Once again, there was somewhere in his mind something he knew was important, but he didn't know what it was.

This time, however, it wasn't a clue he'd failed to notice. It was an issue that involved the Fang Ngil mask – how to find it, or get it, or keep it safe. How to return it to its owner. How to keep it from being sold abroad, to a shady private buyer. For reasons he couldn't quite explain, that morning, before the meeting with Chief Reynolds, he'd decided that he and the others might need a free hand in the issue of the mask, and that telling the Chief too much might prove a mistake.

After all, the Chief was sworn to uphold the law, while he and the other Three Investigators were private consulting detectives, so to speak. As private detectives, they had a different set of priorities and obligations from those of an official police force – and ever since Randy had mentioned that whoever had donated the Fang Ngil mask to Old Art couldn't exactly ask for it back, Jupiter had been worried that there might actually be no legal way to set the situation right.

Now, as he and his friends parked their bikes and went into HQ2, it was Bob who said, "All right. What gives?"

Jupiter frowned. "If we're going to return the Fang Ngil mask to its owner, I think we might have to steal it from wherever it's been taken." His own words surprised him – but only for an instant.

"Steal it?" Pete said. "You mean, as in *steal* it?"

"That's right," Jupiter said. "Remember when Randy said he'd seen the written contract that people who donate stuff to Old Art have to sign? He said it's pretty comprehensive – by which I assume he meant airtight. Also, Julian said that, as far he knew, Old Art had no obligation to sell everything it got from donors within a set period of time.

"In a situation like that, Guadalupe and

Gauthier effectively own the mask already — quite legally — and all they need to do is bide their time. Of course, Kwame Owusu's involvement makes things harder, because if Kwame testified in court and produced the photographs Giovanni Ricci gave him, Old Art would be in big trouble. That's why Guadalupe and Gauthier talked about a hit-and-run."

"But if she's already killed her boss in a hit-and-run," Mallory said, "then surely it would be too risky for her to do that again."

"You'd think so," Jupiter said. "And I inferred that you and Bob believed that Guadalupe and Gauthier weren't entirely serious."

"That's true," Bob said. "They seemed just to be trying the idea on for size."

"They probably were," Jupiter said. "But the problem with the dark triad of personality traits is that when people are manipulative, callous, and immoral, you really never know where and when they will stop. One day they're just con men or women — and the next day they've crossed another line."

"You mean you think they might *really* try to kill Kwame Owusu if they got threatened enough?" Pete asked. "Then wouldn't it be better if we just backed off and didn't do anything at all — much less steal the Fang Ngil mask?"

"It might be," Jupiter said. "But what Old Art is up to – using reverse racism as a cover-up for their fancy forgery and subsequent theft – is really very dangerous. If they were just stealing stuff and getting away with it, it wouldn't cause harm to society as a whole. Well, it would cause *some* harm – but driving a wedge between Hispanics and Asians and African-Americans and people of European descent is causing a whole lot more. If we backed off and did nothing, Old Art would keep causing that harm."

"I *knew* you weren't being totally honest with Chief Reynolds," Bob said suddenly, "and now I can understand why! If we can find the donor and return the Fang Ngil mask, we can promise Old Art a finder's fee or something – but with the proviso that if it gets that, it packs up shop."

"Actually, I hadn't thought that far ahead," Jupiter replied. "I just had the sense that if we let Chief Reynolds know what was really happening at Old Art, it might tie our hands later on. So that idea is all yours, Bob. If we can find both the donor and the Fang Ngil mask, we might be able to convince Giovanni Ricci to stop selling reproductions as if they were the real thing, and force Rémy

Gauthier to go back to Paris."

Since Jupiter hadn't even known these ideas were in his mind ten minutes before, he added, "And if the idea works, I'm giving you full credit for it, Bob."

Bob looked abashed, then smiled.

"Good thinking, Jupe," Pete said. "Except that we have no idea where either the mask or the donor is!"

"As for the mask, I agree with you," Jupiter said. "Though it seems to me at least possible that the mask is at Giovanni Ricci's house. After all, he had to convey it to a place where he could take a series of high-quality photographs and not be interrupted. One of the reasons I asked Mr. Owusu to take us along when he delivers the reproduction was that I'm hoping we can search his house. As for the donor, I've got an idea about that, too, but I don't want to mention it until after we see Peggy Thomas again. Randy and Julian should be here soon."

In fact, they were there five minutes later, and as they wrestled their way out of Randy's Challenger, Jupiter noticed that Julian was holding a fancy paper bag – the kind of bag an upscale bookstore might put a coffee table book in. A big one.

Julian smiled. "I've only borrowed this," he said. "But I thought you might like to see what Uncle Cornelius and Lyle keep in their laundry room."

He reached into the bag and pulled out what Jupiter could see at once was a reproduction of a Fang Ngil mask. To him, it looked rather cheaply made – with machine tooling rather than the painstaking handwork he knew the originals must have exhibited. Nonetheless it had a peculiar power.

It was tall and narrow, chalk white, with deep-set eye slits and an impossibly elongated rectangular nose that ran almost the entire length of the mask. Was it the absence of color that made it so frightening? Jupiter wondered. Or how exaggeratedly stretched it seemed?

"It's really scary," Pete said.

"Yes," said Mallory. "No wonder Lyle jokes about it scaring him into doing the wash."

"He said you could keep it until you found the original," Julian explained.

"Bob, would you put it in HQ2?" Jupiter asked. "Somewhere it won't scare the pants off Uncle Titus if he wanders in there."

Bob grinned, slipped the mask back into the bag, then vanished into Headquarters. When he returned, all six of them piled into a car meant for five, and Jupiter found himself sitting almost in Pete's lap. But while it wasn't the most comfortable ride he'd ever taken, it was certainly fast. In very short order, Randy was driving through the area of Sherman Oaks in which Lyle and Cornelius also had their house, and soon Peggy Thomas was ushering them into her dance studio – where it seemed she was expecting a private dance student soon.

The studio wasn't part of the original house but had been built onto one side of it about thirty years before. Peggy told them it had been a birthday present from Clay – at a time when the two of them had still been rolling in money, as she put it.

When Mallory told her how nice she thought the studio was, Peggy Thomas smiled. "It really is. I'll do everything I can to hang onto it – and not just because it reminds me of Clay, but because I love being able to give dance lessons to children who might otherwise never get them. Julian said you wanted to talk to me about the donation I made to Old Art For Young Artists. What did you want to know?"

"First of all, what the donation was," Jupiter said. If he was right in his hypothesis, now was the moment he would find out. Of course, it was also the moment he would find out if he was wrong.

Luckily, he wasn't.

"I donated three boxes of African masks," Peggy Thomas said. "Clay bought them years ago, in New York, from a cousin of his who had inherited them but who needed some quick money more than he needed art. Clay never really liked them much, and when I was trying to bring myself to give away his clothes – but really couldn't, yet – I thought I'd break myself in slowly by giving away the masks instead."

The minute Peggy Thomas said "African masks" a hush had fallen on the assembled company – a hush so great that the moment Peggy stopped talking, she noticed it.

"What?" she said. "What is it?"

It was Julian who answered – or rather, it was Julian who asked the obvious question.

"Did Clay ever have the masks appraised? For your insurance policy, or anything like that?"

"Not that I know of," Peggy said. "I mean, no, I'm sure he didn't. He'd only paid his cousin a couple of thousand dollars for them, and we never displayed them. I remember one day when he was going through some stuff in the garage, and he found one of the boxes. He said, 'I may be descended from Africans, but this stuff gives me the willies, Peggy.' It gave me the willies, too. That's why I thought it would be a lot easier to say goodbye to it than to give away Clay's clothes!"

"But didn't Old Art get it appraised for you after you'd dropped the stuff off?" Julian asked.

"Yes, they did," Peggy said. "Or at least they gave me the name of an appraiser who went to the warehouse and looked at everything. I was really amazed when he decided that the fifteen masks, taken together, were worth about $50,000! I almost wished I'd sold them instead. But I'll get a really good tax break, and the money from the auction sale will go to deserving young artists. And anyway, $50,000 may sound like a lot of money, but it really wouldn't have made the difference you might think to my future life."

The hush that had fallen had, by now, been replaced by a sense of coiled excitement – excitement so great it seemed to Jupiter almost explosive.

Because he really didn't like explosions very much, he said as calmly as he could, "We think that the appraiser may have been mistaken about the value of at least one of the masks. Could you show us a copy of the appraisal?"

"Of course," Peggy Thomas said, leaving the dance studio. Soon, she was back again and handed Jupiter a sheaf of papers.

Jupiter saw that the appraisal had been done by Sterling Brothers Appraisers in Van Nuys – which Jupiter remembered from the list of approved or suggested appraisal firms on the Old Art website. The masks included a Chokwe mask from the Democratic Republic of Congo and a Dan mask from the Ivory Coast. One of them was marked as a Fang Ngil reproduction of very high quality. But none of the masks was listed with an individual worth.

"Very interesting," he said. "Randy, I think you should show Mrs. Thomas the photographs on your cell phone, and tell her how you got them."

Randy pulled his phone out, swiped it a few times, then held it up so that Peggy Thomas could see.

Yes," she said. "Those are the ones I donated."

"A friend of mine took these pictures in

the Old Art warehouse," he explained. "She knew I know something about African masks. You see that white mask on the far right? I think it may be a real Fang Ngil mask, not a reproduction."

"Really?" Peggy Thomas said, a bit doubtfully.

Randy nodded. "If it's real, it's worth a lot. A *lot*. The thing is, when I asked Hazel to go back and try to get a better picture, she told me that the other masks were still in the warehouse. But the Fang Ngil mask was missing."

"Missing?" asked Peggy. "What do you mean missing?"

"Someone had removed it between the time she took the first picture and the time she went back to take a second one. We don't know where it is now, so we can't know for certain if it's authentic."

"But wouldn't the appraiser know whether it was real or not?" Peggy asked in bewilderment.

"Not necessarily," Julian said. "A lot of appraisers are generalists, and this would be a job for a specialist. Anyway, we're almost certain the missing mask *is* real, because Giovanni Ricci hired a craftsman from Ghana to make a reproduction Fang Ngil mask from a set of photographs. We think Old Art plans to sell that mask at the auction, then sell the real mask later and keep the profits.”

Peggy Thomas looked as if she were having trouble taking in everything she was being told. When Jupiter said, “Would you like to get some water?” she said, “Yes, let’s go into the house.”

Soon, they were sitting in her living room.

“Excuse me,” she said. “I think I should cancel my dance lesson; I need to make a phone call.”

When she came back, she seemed more composed. In fact, she suddenly seemed a bit excited. “I guess I could look at this as a blessing,” she said. “Although the mask being missing isn’t great. And I think I signed a piece of paper giving up all rights to the masks when I dropped them off. But surely that wouldn’t hold up in court if it could be proved that they were actually trying to steal donations which had been intended to profit the underprivileged?”

“Since none of us are lawyers, we don’t really know,” Jupiter said. “But if you’d be willing to appoint The Three Investigators as your representatives, maybe we can find a solution to the problem. I assume from what you just said that if you could get the mask back, you'd keep it, or sell it yourself?"

"I certainly would," Peggy Thomas said. "I'd keep it long enough to sell it. Randy didn't say what he thought it might be worth, and I imagine that with things that are hard to appraise, it must be hard to guess what something might bring at auction. But I can tell you this: If The Three Investigators can get the mask back to me, then whatever it sells for, I'll be giving you a percentage of it. I'd love to see four such amazing young people re-stock their coffers!"

But even though Jupiter would have loved that, too, at the moment his attention was focused solely on getting the mask back.

Peggy Thomas went on. "And, you know, once I knew I had enough money to stay in my house, I think what I'd like to do with the rest is set up a foundation of my own. One that did what Old Art For Young Artists just pretends to do – help young people to learn about, or do, art."

"What a good idea," Randy said. "But what Jupiter hasn't said yet is that he thinks it may be necessary to actually steal the mask to get it back. If he can find it first, of course!"

"But wouldn't that be dangerous?" asked Peggy.

"It might," Jupiter admitted. "But if you'd be willing to give us a written commission to recover the piece, I don't think we'd have to worry about the legality of it. Not that it would really be legal to steal it. Just that under the circumstances, I don't think the police would be eager to prosecute."

"That's good," Peggy said. "But it wasn't what I meant. I meant that if these people are as criminal as they seem to be, you might be in physical danger. And no matter how much the mask is worth, it wouldn't be worth *that*!"

"We'll be careful," Jupiter said. "And we have more experience with danger than you might think."

Peggy looked at him appraisingly. "I'll write you a formal commission right now," she said. When she had, Jupiter tucked it into his pocket and shook her hand.

Soon afterwards, Randy was driving them all back to Rocky Beach. Pete was due at the Rescue Center and Mallory had promised Jupiter's Aunt Mathilda she'd put in a few hour's work.

Before Bob left to go home, he and Jupiter talked about the possibility that they really *would* find the missing mask.

Just then, the phone on the desk of HQ2 rang. Jupiter dashed over and punched the speakerphone button.

"Three Investigators Headquarters. Jupiter Jones speaking," he said.

A deep, lilting voice said, "This is Kwame Owusu. Mr. Ricci has asked me to deliver the mask tomorrow night at 8:00."

"You've finished it, then?" Jupiter asked.

"Oh, yes," Mr. Owusu said. "It is very beautiful. I will pick you and your friends up at 7:15. That will give us plenty of time to get there."

"We'll be ready," Jupiter assured him.

"I was thinking," Mr. Owusu said. "If the four of you are to be my interns, maybe you should look alike."

"Like we're wearing a uniform?" Bob asked.

"Yes!" Mr. Owusu said. "Like a uniform. A dark one, if you can."

"I'm afraid that may be difficult," Jupiter said.

"No, it won't," Bob said. "We all have black clothes, and everyone knows that artists dress in black." He grinned at Jupiter. "We all have a black shirt or t-shirt, and dark pants – very dark jeans."

"Black uniforms would be very good," Mr. Owusu said. "And there is something I think I should tell you. I believe that you and Bob are on a speakerphone?"

"We are," Jupiter confirmed.

"When Mr. Ricci called me, he was on a speakerphone, too. I think he was in his studio. An artist in his studio likes to have both hands free."

"I imagine that's true," Jupiter said. "But why do you bring it up?"

"Because when Mrs. Ricci came into the studio I don't think she knew Mr. Ricci was on the phone. She talked as if they were alone together. She was laughing, but she said something about a mask that gave her what she called the heebie-jeebies. She said she didn't want the baby to see it when he was born – that it wasn't a teddy bear or a stuffed lion! That's all I heard, because Mr. Ricci picked up the handset. But to me, it sounded as if Mr. Ricci had the mask right there in his home."

"Could he have been referring to the mask you're making for him?" Jupiter asked. "He might have shown her the photographs he gave you."

"That is possible," Mr. Owusu said. "But it sounded to me as if she'd seen something real, not just a photograph. That's why I thought you should wear the uniforms. So you'd be harder to tell apart if you had a chance to search the house."

"Excellent thinking," Jupiter said. "I'd already been hoping we might get that chance. In the meantime, you'll be interested to know that we've found the person who donated the African masks to Old Art For Young Artists. She's a woman named Peggy Thomas − a dancer who inherited the mask from her husband, who recently died. And she's given The Three Investigators formal permission to try to get her mask back. To steal it, if necessary."

"It wouldn't be stealing if it was hers to begin with!" said Mr. Owusu sternly. "Please be dressed and ready to go at 7:15 tomorrow."

"We will be," Bob said.

Jupiter punched the speakerphone off. "Kwame Owusu is proving an excellent addition to the team," he said. "But if we really want to search Giovanni Ricci's house while we're there, we'll have to create a diversion. A big one."

As he spoke, he noticed the bag containing the reproduction Fang Ngil mask Julian had borrowed from his uncle. He took out the mask and gazed at it thoughtfully.

"Quite a scary fellow," he said. "I wonder if there's a way we could use it tomorrow night."

"What do you mean?" Bob asked.

"If Giovanni Ricci knows about Fang Ngil masks," Jupiter said, "then he certainly knows their history. What if a member of the Fang Ngil were to show up at Ricci's house, the way members of the secret society would appear under cover of darkness to scare evildoers straight?"

Bob looked at him as if he thought he'd lost his mind.

"I'm serious," Jupiter said. "After all, we'll be getting there just as it's starting to get dark, and if we're all dressed in black −. Maybe Pete shouldn't come with us when we go into Ricci's house with Mr. Owusu. Maybe he should burst in later, after we're all inside. He could say something in a weird voice about how he knows what Ricci is up to and how he won't get away with it. The rest of us could quickly search the house."

"I don't know," Bob said. "Having Pete burst in might create a brief diversion, but it wouldn't last long. It might be better to kill the lights. Or kill the lights first, and then have Pete do his thing. He could shine a flashlight on the mask."

"I like your idea about the lights," Jupiter said.

He pinched his bottom lip again. "If we can get access to the electrical panel, with its breakers, we can turn off all the electricity in the house by flipping a single switch. I doubt that Ricci's house has a basement, so it'll be on the ground floor somewhere, probably in a utility closet. One of us will have to find it and flip the switch while the rest of us are keeping Ricci and his wife occupied."

"But if Pete's outside and we're inside," Bob asked, "how are we going to stay in touch? We can't use our walkie-talkies because of the static – plus it would be awkward to have to push the button."

"Hmm," Jupiter said. "That's a tough one."

"Maybe I could give Pete my phone and Mallory could call him and then keep an open line between the two."

"That's an excellent idea, Bob," Jupiter said.

Jupiter found he was oddly pleased with the plan – all of them dressed as cat burglars and Pete bursting in with the Fang Ngil mask and a flashlight, while the rest of them searched the house after the lights went out.

"We should all have flashlights, of course," he said. "We can pull them out when we've cut the electricity. Of course we can't know for sure this will work, but it might. Why don't you go to the shed Mallory's working in and fill her in on the details? I'll call Pete and give him the news."

Bob smiled. "You'll like that, won't you?" he said.

"Indeed I will," Jupiter said. "But I doubt I'll like it more than Pete does! And I think Mallory is going to like this plan, too!"

14

Into The Lion's Den

"What's with the black clothes?" Mallory's mother asked as she passed the potatoes early the following evening. Mallory and her mother were eating dinner in the dining room of their apartment at the Wessex House, and Mallory was wondering whether she should have waited until after they ate to change into her all-black uniform. Mallory took the potatoes and put a spoonful on her plate but didn't answer her mother's question. Instead, she shrugged and smiled, as if she didn't know the answer.

She hadn't seen her mother much recently. They'd been on different paths – Mallory finishing up the design and renovation of HQ2, working for Aunt Mathilda, and starting the first Three Investigators case of the summer, and her mother with her work as a costume designer and her relationship with Bobby Woodruff.

Woodruff was a fellow costume designer who her mother had been seeing for a year or so before she'd finally broken it off with him, just a few weeks before. He'd been a bit of a stick insect – or at least a very low-energy man, and one who'd annoyed Mallory so much that she'd been rude to him on a number of memorable occasions.

However, one good thing had come out of the relationship – or at least out of the breakup. The night Mallory's mother had told Woodruff she didn't want to see him any more, she'd been so upset she'd cried in her bedroom after arriving back from her date. Mallory had heard her crying and had gone to find out what was wrong.

She didn't think of herself as a maternal sort of person, but when someone was crying, alone in the dark, it would be inhuman not to see if you could help them. And as it turned out, she *had* helped, because when her mother had told her what had happened, she added that sometimes she missed Mallory's father so much she could hardly bear it. Since she almost never said anything like that, it had really softened Mallory's heart, and she had found herself telling her mother not to worry – that the right man would come along one day.

Her mother had been very grateful – so grateful that as Mallory lay next to her on her big double bed, Mallory had finally told her plainly that she wanted to stay in Rocky Beach for good. When they'd first arrived, Mallory had hated California, and her mother had promised her that if she'd just give the place a try – but for two whole years! – if she found she didn't like it, they'd move back to Scotland.

The two years were now up, and Mallory had long ago decided that she wanted to stay. But even though anyone with eyes could have seen that, her mother had needed to have Mallory tell her outright, and finally she had.

"You don't know how glad I am to hear you say that," her mother had said, reaching out to take Mallory's hand. "I would have taken you back to Scotland if you'd wanted to go, but I really didn't want to. Too many memories."

Mallory had often thought that her mother didn't grieve for her father the way she did. But clearly she'd been wrong, and ever since that evening, she and her mother had been getting along much better.

Now, however, she was wishing she hadn't changed into her all-black clothes, because they were making her mother very curious about The Three Investigators' plans for the evening, and even though Mallory didn't think they would be in any danger at the Riccis' house, her mother worried about stuff like this.

And, anyway, you never knew.

"No, really, why black clothes?" her mother asked again. This time, Mallory decided to tell her what was going on.

"We're all going to be wearing black," she said. "There's this artist from Ghana who's been making a piece on commission for a nonprofit foundation called Old Art For Young Artists, and the four of us are going to pretend to be his interns."

"Pretend to whom?" her mother asked.

"The guy who commissioned the piece," Mallory said. "Kwame Owusu is delivering it to him tonight and we're going with him, because we're investigating the nonprofit. They're running a very elaborate scam, and we're trying to prove it."

"So where are you going? To the offices of the foundation?" Mallory's mother asked.

"No," Mallory said. "To the house of one of the directors. He's an artist himself, and he's married to a set designer."

"Really?" Mallory's mother said. "I wonder if I know her."

"I doubt it," said Mallory. "Though Pete's father does. He said she was a lovely woman."

"What's her name?" Mallory's mother

252

asked.

"Alyssa Ricci," Mallory said. "But she's five months pregnant, so I doubt she's working much these days."

To Mallory's great surprise, her mother's face lit up.

"I know Alyssa! Or at least I've met her. She's African-American, isn't she? And you're wrong, she actually *is* working – on a movie I did a special commission for. She was there the day I delivered it, and I met her. We ended up sitting together while I waited for the art director to show up, and when I asked her about the baby, she told me a funny story. She said that she and her husband had recently watched Steven Spielberg's movie *E.T.* – about the alien who comes to earth and gets left behind? They saw it for the first time ever.

"Alyssa said something about how being pregnant made her interested in all these old movies made for children, and that she and her husband had loved it. There was one scene they really laughed at – the one where E.T. hides in the little boy's closet and surrounds himself with plush toys and stuffed animals, and when the mother looks in the closet, E.T. is perfectly camouflaged and she doesn't even notice him. Remember that scene?"

Mallory did remember it, but she remembered even more clearly another scene in which Elliott's sister Gertie dressed up E.T. with a raffia wig and beads, and how Mallory had thought it was pretty disrespectful. But funny.

"Anyway, I liked her," Mallory's mother concluded, "and I hope you're wrong about her husband."

"I'm not wrong," Mallory said. "But from what we can tell, he really loves his wife, and we're hoping that maybe we can find a way to put an end to the fraud and theft and deception by appealing to his better nature."

Or by stealing the mask he's hidden in his house somewhere, Mallory thought.

She glanced at her watch and saw that it was already 6:30. She'd promised to clean up the kitchen, and then it would be time to bike to the Salvage Yard. By the time the dishes were loaded into the dishwasher, and the pots and pans washed, dried, and put away, it was time to leave. She said goodbye to her mother, buckled her helmet on, and jumped on her bike. When she got to the Salvage Yard, Mr. Owusu was already there, and since the boys had taken the back seat in the extended cab of his truck, Mallory climbed in front with him.

He seemed very excited. When she asked him where he'd put the mask he'd made, he told her it was carefully wrapped and in the back, under the truck cap.

The boys were in high spirits, especially Pete. He had the imitation Fang Ngil mask which Julian Jackson had borrowed from Lyle and Cornelius in his lap, and he seemed delighted with the part he'd get to play in the evening's drama. He kept holding it up to his face and then returning it to his lap, and practicing holding the flashlight at the bottom of the mask, shining up.

"How's this?" he asked. He shifted the flashlight. "Is this better?"

The first way was better, Mallory thought. But it made little difference. Either way, it was very spooky. Though she knew it was Pete, it was still disconcerting to see the mask in the stark white of the flashlight's beam. Under the smooth protruding forehead, the slitted sunken eyes and cheeks were in shadow, while the long nose caught the light. It looked like a death mask, and it filled Mallory with foreboding.

"You're going to freak the hell out of the Riccis," Bob said.

"Really?" Pete said, grinning.

"Oh, yes," Jupiter said. "Or at least Mr. Ricci."

"Why not both of them?" Mallory asked.

"Because after what Mr. Owusu over-heard her saying about the mask scaring her, I doubt very much she'll be in the house when we get there. After all, if we're right that Mr. Ricci has been trying to keep her from understanding what he and his partners at Old Art are actually up to — and if she's seen the original Fang Ngil mask — then surely her husband won't want her to see Mr. Owusu's reproduction."

"You're right," Bob said. "It would be a dead giveaway!"

"Of course," Mallory said.

"Let's make sure we have everything in place," Jupiter went on. "First, synchronize your watches. By my time it's … 7:43."

Mallory was off by a minute and adjusted her watch.

"Now, about staying in touch," Jupiter said. "Bob, why don't you give Pete your phone now? We can establish contact when Pete gets out. Pete, it's very important that you not make any unnecessary noise on your end while the line's open. Remember what happened when Mr. Ricci was on speakerphone and Mrs. Ricci came into the room while he was talking with

Mr. Owusu."

"Yes," Kwame Owusu said. "It is always a hazard in our modern world. That people will overhear what they aren't meant to. And not always on a telephone. Sometimes through a door."

As Mallory looked sideways, she saw that he was smiling slightly, and she suddenly realized that he must have heard what Jupiter had been talking about the day he came to their new Headquarters – that at the Gala, Juanita Guadalupe had said that if he got wind of what they were up to, they might have to take drastic action.

As Mallory remembered, Jupiter had said that, whatever they did, they shouldn't scare Kwame Owusu by telling him that part of the story. But now it seemed that he hadn't been scared at all!

"You heard!" Pete said.

"I heard," said Mr. Owusu. "But when you're making a reproduction Fang Ngil mask, you don't scare easy!" He drove another block or two. "We're getting close now," he said. "Do you want me to let Pete out here?"

"That's a great idea," Jupiter said.

Mr. Owusu pulled to the curb, and Pete and Mallory turned their phones on.

"Testing, one, two, three," Pete said. "Testing ... "

"Pete, you're testing *me*," Jupiter said. "Do you have the address?" Pete nodded. "O.K., then. We're on."

Pete got out of the car, juggling the mask, the flashlight, and the phone. On his back he was wearing an empty black rucksack into which he planned to put the imitation mask if he had the chance to search the house after the diversion. He looked excited. Everyone waved to him as the truck rolled on.

They reached the Riccis' house in no time, and Mallory was surprised at how suburban, how low-key and pleasant, the neighborhood was. The houses were crowded together on smallish lots. The Riccis' was a large and well-maintained ranch, with a low-pitch gable roof, nearly flat. Mallory caught a glimpse of a swing set in the back yard – they were really planning ahead!

Mr. Owusu went to the back of the truck and took out the carefully wrapped mask he'd made. Then leading the way, with Mallory, Bob, and Jupiter right behind him in their black outfits, he walked up to the door and rang the bell. As Jupiter had predicted, it was Giovanni Ricci who answered the door.

Up close, he was just as handsome as he had seemed from a distance at the Gala – but tonight he was dressed in a jacket and tie and he looked quite tired, even haggard. He frowned as he looked past Kwame Owusu to see Jupiter, Bob, and Mallory. He didn't say anything, but he looked at Mr. Owusu with a question in his eyes.

"These three young people are my interns," Mr. Owusu said. "I hope you don't mind my bringing them."

"Not at all," Mr. Ricci said, gesturing for them to come in. "Though I wasn't aware you *had* interns."

"Oh, yes," said Kwame Owusu. "They didn't help me with the mask, of course, but they watched me while I made it."

"Did they?" asked Mr. Ricci with sudden uneasiness. "Why don't you take the mask to the dining room and unpack it on the table there?"

Mallory followed along as Mr. Owusu did as he'd been asked. The Riccis' house seemed warm and hospitable. The light apricot walls were hung with paintings, and the throw cushions on the sofas were highly elaborate – embroidered, quilted, or appliquéd. While Mr. Owusu began to carefully unwrap the mask he had made, Mallory studied one of the paintings on the living room wall. It featured a young woman with an elongated neck and a wistful face. If Mallory hadn't known better, she would have sworn it was a Modigliani.

As for Kwame Owusu's mask, it was quite big – two feet long and both narrow and deep, with a wide bare forehead that led to a small stylized cap. Mallory saw that the dome of the skull was large enough so that the Fang Ngil member who'd worn it could have balanced it on top of his head, leaving his hands free. It was very beautiful and strange, Mallory thought. She was quite impressed with Mr. Owusu's work, but she refrained from saying that. After all, Mr. Owusu had just told Giovanni Ricci that she and Bob and Jupiter had watched while he made it.

Even so, she couldn't keep herself from saying, "It's very impressive, isn't it?"

Giovanni Ricci looked at her keenly. "It certainly is," he said. "If I didn't know better, I might think this was an original." Almost tenderly, he lifted the mask up so that he could see it from the top and bottom, and the back, and to Mallory it seemed as if he was truly impressed by its artistry.

Maybe Giovanni Ricci was a good guy

after all, Mallory thought – someone who'd just gotten himself entangled with a bad companion from his student days. Maybe what he'd said at the Gala was true – that he saw the sale of the Fang Ngil mask as a way to break free and start clean.

It was almost dark outside, almost time to put their plan in motion. Mallory patted her phone, still open in her shirt pocket, and she wondered what Pete had made of whatever he'd managed to hear. On his end, he'd been totally quiet.

As Giovanni Ricci continued to examine the reproduction mask, Jupiter asked if he could use the bathroom. Mr. Ricci nodded and directed him down a hall. Mallory knew he was really looking for the electrical panel and thought he'd chosen a good time to excuse himself, while everyone else watched Ricci as he examined the mask he'd commissioned.

He set the mask back on the dining room table and said to Mr. Owusu, "It's amazing. Really perfect."

"I am so happy you are pleased," Mr. Owusu said.

There was that moment of silence that falls on a group when no one can think of what to say next, and the silence becomes tense and everyone seizes up. But Mr. Owusu saved the day.

"I am sorry your wife is not here tonight. I so enjoyed meeting her the first time I came. You and she must be so excited about the baby. I have two children, a boy and a girl, and soon we will all be American citizens together. And my wife, of course. Children change everything, you know."

Giovanni Ricci smiled.

"That's what I'm told," he said. He reached into his pants pocket and pulled out a wad of bills. "Let me pay you the rest of the money I owe you," he said. He counted out what Mallory assumed must have been two thousand dollars. Mr. Owusu thanked him and put it in his wallet. Mallory was starting to get worried that if Jupiter didn't get back to the dining room quickly, their whole plan might be blown. But before the silence could grow long, Mr. Owusu saved the day again.

"When I was driving up your driveway, I saw that you have a swing set! Already!" he said. "You are planning ahead, I see. And do you have a separate room for the baby? A nursery? In Ghana, babies sleep with their mothers, in the same bed, and when they are a little older, they sleep on a mat on the floor.

But when they are ten, they go sleep with their older brothers and sisters in another room."

He smiled and shook his head.

"When my wife and I were in Ghana, we thought that was a fine way to do things, but now that I am in America, I like that my children can have their own room and not take up so much of the bed!" He laughed.

But although all this talking about babies had bought The Three Investigators some time, Mr. Owusu couldn't talk forever, Mallory thought. She'd noticed that when Mr. Owusu had asked about the nursery, Giovanni Ricci had tensed up and looked almost agitated.

All of a sudden she remembered the Gala, when Alyssa Ricci had joined her husband and had talked about fixing up the nursery and buying lots of toys – and also her mother's story about how Alyssa and her husband had laughed at the scene in *E.T.* in which E.T. had hidden in the bedroom among the dolls and stuffed animals.

Could Ricci have taken the movie to heart when he'd been looking for a place to hide the authentic Fang Ngil mask?

When Bob had told her about the plan for tonight, he'd reported what Mr. Owusu had said about overhearing Mrs. Ricci. Was it possible that that was what she'd been referring to when she'd told her husband that she didn't want the baby to see the mask? What else had she said? Mallory wondered. She had to get a look at the Riccis' nursery before another moment passed!

She excused herself to use the bathroom, too, and strode confidently down the hall, peering left and right into the rooms she passed. There was Jupiter coming toward her, finally. As he brushed past, she asked, under her breath, "Did you find the circuit breaker?"

"Yes," Jupiter whispered. "Utility closet. End of the hall. Around the corner, on the right. Across from the bathroom. Where are you going?"

"I'm trying to find the nursery," Mallory whispered back. "As far as I can remember, my mother has never given me a single good idea about any of our investigations, but this time, she just might have. I'll tell you about it later. Just keep Ricci talking for as long as you possibly can."

Mallory kept walking down the hall, enchanted with her surmise. She found the nursery near the end, on the left, opposite the master bedroom, and, without entering it yet, she glanced in. The window stood open to the evening air, and white eyelet curtains ruffled in the light breeze. The walls had been papered in bright colors, with moons and suns and shooting stars. In the corner was a bassinet on casters, next to a small crib with pine slats. The warm glow of a yellow night light suffused the room. All that was missing was the baby.

Mallory looked behind her up the hall, then found the bathroom and the utility closet Jupiter had discovered. Very cautiously, she opened it to see how easy it would be to cut off the electricity for the entire house. She suddenly had a brand-new idea – one which wouldn't involve Pete bursting into the house holding the Fang Ngil mask in front of his face, but which might be far more effective at achieving their actual goal.

She closed the door of the utility closet, took her flashlight out of her pocket, looked behind her up the hall again, and returned to the nursery. This time, she darted in. At the far end was what had to be the nursery closet, with louvered doors.

As she walked toward it, she saw that the window sill wasn't more than three feet above the ground. Although there were streetlights on the streets they'd driven through to get here, none of them could be seen from this corner of the house. So far, so good, she thought.

Carefully, slowly – trying to make as little noise as possible – she eased the closet doors open and peered inside. A cedar rod stretched from one side to the other. Mallory saw that the Riccis had stored their winter coats and rain gear in here. She pushed them aside as quietly as she could to reveal a series of built-in shelves.

The Riccis were thinking ahead, all right. The shelves were already stuffed with toys and dolls – Raggedy Anns and Raggedy Andys, plush bears, china dolls with dark painted faces, stuffed bunnies and ducks, an otter, a stuffed lion, and –

The hair on the back of Mallory's neck stood on end, and she gasped. There, among the toys and stuffed animals, partially hidden, was the Fang Ngil mask. Mr. Owusu had done a marvelous job of copying it from photographs, but his was a reproduction. The original had an aura of menace unlike anything Mallory had ever experienced. It had a blankness about it, a disquieting stillness that made its chalky whiteness truly frightening. Its small, cupped ears were emblazoned with arrows burned into the wood and pointing toward the eyes.

The eyes – . The eyes were narrow rectangular slits, totally unlike the soft almond liquidity of human eyes. These were eyes from beyond the grave. Giovanni Ricci had tried to disguise what he had hidden in the nursery closet with a raffia wig and several loops of pop beads, but none of that could hide what was there.

In fact, instead of making the Fang Ngil mask look antic, the fake hair and pop beads managed to emphasize its essential spookiness. It had an otherworldly power that seemed to throw a spell over Mallory. She could feel her skin prickle as if a cold wind had just blown across her. The glare of her flashlight made the mask blaze. This was the real thing, she knew.

She stepped backward into the nursery and closed her eyes. Her heart was racing. She could hear the sound of conversation coming from the living room. As she took her phone out of her pocket, she was thinking hard.

15

An Almost Perfectly Executed Plan

Pete stood behind the trunk of a tree, about fifty feet from the Riccis' house, holding Bob's phone up to his ear with one hand. He'd been trying to listen to the conversation inside the house, but too many of the voices were muffled and he kept losing the thread.

Frustrated and a bit jittery, he held the imitation Fang Ngil mask up to his face with the other hand, letting it hang from the crown of his head. Sure enough, it stayed there on its own. But as excited as he was about the idea of shocking Giovanni Ricci, he'd begun to doubt Jupiter's plan. It was fun, all right, but he really didn't know where it was going to get them. After all, Ricci was an Italian, not a Fang, and instead of scaring him or throwing him off balance, to have Pete jump into his house with a mask on might simply make him angry.

When Mallory and the others first arrived, Pete had been happy to learn that Jupiter was right – that Mrs. Ricci wasn't in the house. Whatever happened – or didn't – he didn't want her in the middle of it. Especially if the lights really went off. But would they? And if so, when?

So far, he'd heard that the mask had been presented to Giovanni Ricci and that Mr. Ricci had paid Kwame Owusu for his work. He'd also heard Mallory say she was leaving the room – after which there had been a brief interchange with Jupiter and then silence. Listening to the silence was even more nerve-wracking than trying to piece together fragments of conversation had been.

Then, all of a sudden, he heard Mallory's voice – and not faraway as it had been before, muffled by her pocket, but clearly and distinctly, as if she were holding it up to her mouth and speaking into it.

"Pete?" she said. "Are you there? You can talk. Just keep it low."

"Yeah," he said. "I'm here."

"How close are you?" Mallory asked.

"I'm behind a tree in the next-door neighbor's front yard," Pete said. "I've been keeping an eye on the house. Where are you?"

"I'm in the Riccis' nursery," Mallory said. "I'm alone."

"I figured," Pete said. "What are you doing there?"

"I had a hunch," Mallory said. "Jupiter and Bob don't know it yet, but I've found the mask. It's here, in the nursery closet. Ricci tried to disguise it, but it's hiding in plain sight."

"Wow!" Pete said. "Is it cool?"

"It's scary," said Mallory. "Wait 'til you see it. Listen. I had what I think is a good idea."

"Yeah?" Pete said.

"Since I've already found the mask, I think we should move directly to cutting the lights, then stealing it. There's no way I can clear this with Jupiter and Bob, because when I go back to the living room, everyone will be able to hear me. But under the circumstances, it makes a lot more sense for you to climb into the nursery window when the lights go off than it does for you to burst in the front door with a flashlight on your face."

"I see what you mean," Pete said. "The plan made sense when we didn't know where the mask was, but now that we do − . I just hope I can find it and get it out of the house without dropping it or something!"

"You won't drop it," Mallory said. "The nursery window is already open. I'll nudge it as far up as I can. Just grab the mask and get yourself out of the house again."

"How will I know the right room?" Pete said. "What if there are other windows open?"

"It's at the far end of the house, at the back. It's got long white curtains in the window. You can't miss it. And the street lamps from the street don't shine in this corner of the yard. Once I turn the lights off, no one will see you climbing into or out of the window."

"Are you leaving the mask in the closet?" Pete asked.

"I haven't touched it," Mallory said. "You should bring Lyle and Cornelius's mask and switch them. Take your time and make the reproduction look as much like the original as you can. I mean, at the moment it's got a raffia wig and pop beads on it."

Pete laughed. "You're kidding," he said.

"It seems that Mr. Ricci took his inspiration from a scene in *E.T.*"

"That's wild," Pete said.

"Just make it so that anyone sneaking a glance into the closet won't notice that anything's different," Mallory said. "Then climb back outside and take the mask around the corner with you. Walk as fast as you can. Wait for us to pick you up."

"We should have a code of some sort," Pete said. "Some signal I can give you to let you know I got the mask and that I'm safely down the street. That will let you know you should get out of the house and come find me."

"Great idea," Mallory said. "What do you think it should be?"

"How about 'E.T. phone home'?" Pete suggested. "Like what Gordon Small thought Daniel Barnes had said when he was trying to call Etuis Ceriph!"

"I don't think that's a very good idea," Mallory said. "Wait! Ssshhh! I think I hear footsteps!"

Oh, no, Pete thought. If Mallory was caught in the nursery what would she say? How would she explain it? She was a good actor, but if Ricci discovered her, they'd be in trouble. He strained to hear but there was nothing but silence.

"No," Mallory finally said. "We're fine. It must have been my imagination. I'm a little jumpy."

"You're jumpy?" Pete said. "I feel like a Mexican jumping bean. If I'm allowed to say that any more."

"You're allowed to," she said.

"So back to the signal," Pete said. "You don't like 'E.T. phone home.'"

"It would stick out too much," Mallory

said. "Call attention to itself. And to the mask in the nursery closet. How about just an ordinary word that anyone could have said for any reason?"

The image of the huge screen-filling moon came to Pete, with Elliott on his bicycle in silhouette, and E.T. in his basket.

"How about 'bicycle'?" Pete asked.

"Bicycle it is," Mallory said.

"Are you going to cut the lights?" Pete asked.

"Just as soon as we get off the phone," Mallory said. "But be sure to keep the line open in case something unforeseen happens."

"Got it," Pete said. "I will. How else would I say 'bicycle', anyway?"

Mallory laughed. "O.K.," she said. "Let's do it. Bye."

Pete put Bob's phone in his shirt pocket, grabbed the reproduction Fang Ngil mask, and stopped dead. It suddenly occurred to ask himself – it was too late to ask Mallory – if he was going to be trespassing. He knew Jupiter always said that if a door was open, you could walk through it. But what about a window? He wouldn't be breaking anything, but he would be entering.

Of course, that paled in comparison to

taking something that didn't belong to him out of someone else's house. That was clearly theft. Although since Peggy Thomas had appointed The Three Investigators as her agents for the recovery of her property, Pete hoped it would come out all right in the end.

He tucked the imitation Fang Ngil mask under his arm and darted to the end of the house, glad that Kwame Owusu had suggested that his interns should wear black tonight. He was walking very slowly and carefully around the house, looking for an open window, when suddenly all the lights in the house went off. Although Pete had been expecting this, he still jumped when it happened, and from inside the house he heard exclamations of surprise and dismay.

All right, he thought. Time to hurry. He worked his way down the back of the house. Mallory had been right that the street lamps didn't illuminate anything back here, and since it was dark outside as well as in, he tried to see where he put his feet in the darkness. He didn't want to fall or bark his shin or cry out suddenly. He came to an open window and was about to hoist himself up when he remembered that Mallory had said the nursery had white curtains, while this room had blinds. So he kept going.

About twenty feet further on, he came to another open window. Flimsy white curtains hung in the space. This had to be it.

As quietly as he could, he jumped and pushed himself up with his arms, clamping down on the mask in his armpit to keep it from falling. That hurt – so much he thought he'd have to let go. But somehow he managed to maneuver one leg over the sill and into the room, and sitting there, with his leg inside and his torso outside, he managed to reach up and get the mask in his hand.

"Oww," he said quietly.

He swiveled, wiggled, and managed to swing his other leg over the sill until he was finally in the room. It was even darker inside than out.

He stopped to listen. Up the hall in the living room people were talking over one another. He thought he heard the word "hairdryer," but that made little sense. He realized he had no time to waste. Ricci would soon go looking for the electrical service panel and would see that the master switch had flipped.

He took his small tactical flashlight from his pocket and turned it on. Cupping his hand over the lens to mask the light, he crept toward the closet. The louvered doors stood open, just as Mallory had left them. When he shone his light in, he saw that Mallory had swept aside the raincoats and jackets and overcoats that hung from the cedar rod. In the recesses of the closet, he saw the stuffed animals and toys.

And there, wearing a raffia wig and strands of pink pop beads, was the mask. It stared straight ahead, stern, implacable. In the movie, E.T.'s face, which was the only part of him showing, blended in quite well with the stuffed animals. But nothing could make the Fang Ngil mask look like anything other than what it was. It was fundamentally undisguisable, Pete thought.

Carefully, he picked it up from where it had been wedged between a stuffed lion and a large polar bear and carefully removed the pop beads and the wig. The mask was surprisingly heavy and considerably larger than the mask they'd borrowed from Lyle and Cornelius.

It suddenly occurred to him that they would probably never get their mask back if he left it in this closet, and he felt bad about that – though only for an instant. He placed the real mask on the floor at his feet, then took the one he'd brought with him and positioned it between the lion and the bear. Then he looped the pop beads around it and tried to arrange the raffia so that it covered much of the face. Although Lyle and Cornelius's mask and the original were very different, Pete satisfied himself that someone just glancing in might be fooled.

He picked up the Fang Ngil mask, and all at once it struck him that he was holding something that might be worth five million dollars. The thought stunned him. He couldn't even imagine the idea of that much money or the fact that this hand-carved representation of a human face could be worth that.

As he backed out of the closet, his sneaker caught on an uneven piece of flooring and he stumbled backwards, dropping the flashlight, which clattered on the floor and sent its beam careening from wall to ceiling. He had two simultaneous thoughts – he had to keep himself from falling and he had to protect the mask. He managed to keep his balance, but he froze, afraid the racket that he and the flashlight had made would bring someone running. If so, what to do? Dive into the closet, closing the doors behind him? Or dive through the window?

He stooped and picked up the flashlight and covered it with his palm. His hand glowed golden-red, like E.T.'s finger. As he stood there holding his breath, it became clear that he didn't have to dive anywhere. The voices in the living room continued at the same level. He let out his breath.

Swiftly he went back into the closet to check his work. The raffia wig and the pop beads were just as he'd left them. He quickly rearranged the outerwear so that it was evenly spaced on the rod and hid the closet's interior. Someone would have to sweep them aside in order to see the mask. Then he closed the louvered doors and crept back across the room to the open window.

Even now, when he was almost finished – or maybe especially now – he felt naked and exposed, as if he could be caught out at any moment. He wondered how burglars did it, how they managed to deal with the adrenaline and the nerves. In the movies, this sort of thing always looked so easy and sort of fun. Thieves dangled from bungee cords and evaded laser beams. Well, it wasn't easy at all, Pete thought, even without any of those complications. And it certainly wasn't fun.

He pocketed his flashlight. Now the trick was how to get back out the window without damaging or breaking the mask. That would just be Pete's luck! He could see the headline in the Los Angeles *Sun*. IDIOT TEENAGER BREAKS PRICELESS ART OBJECT DURING ATTEMPTED THEFT. There would be his mug shot next to a picture of the ruined mask. He'd have destroyed one of only twelve or so masks of its kind in the whole entire world.

He gulped and shook his head to rid it of these dark thoughts. Carefully, holding the mask in both hands, he leaned out the window, then balanced his hips on the sill. Using them as a fulcrum and his body like a seesaw, he slowly tilted forward. The hard sharp wood cut into his belly, and for a sickening moment, he felt himself slipping. But then his belt caught on the windowsill and held him firm. He reached out as far as he could and was just able to set the Fang Ngil mask on the grass.

Then, as quickly as he could, he unhooked his belt from the sill and slithered out the window. Phew! He felt a surge of exaltation as he hurried from the back of the house to the sidewalk in front of it, the mask firmly clamped under his left arm. Now all he had to do was get far enough away and say "bicycle" to Mallory. He patted his shirt pocket and a jolt of cold fear ran through him. The phone was missing.

He panicked. Where had it gone? Had he ever taken it out of his pocket? His mind felt so scrambled that he just couldn't remember. He thought he might hyperventilate, and then he started talking to himself. Calm down, Pete, he said. You can do this. Think!

And then it came to him. The phone must have fallen out of his shirt pocket when he'd been tipping forward out the window, holding the mask. keeping the mask secured. It must be on the lawn under the nursery window. He set the mask down on the grass for a second time, took his flashlight back out of his pocket and cupped the light again. Stealthily but as quickly as possible, he stole back down the length of the house. His heart was in his throat, but there, glinting in the flashlight's beam, was Bob's cell phone.

Miraculously, it had fallen without shutting, and the line was still open. When he held it to his ear, he could hear the people in the living room still arguing.

What luck! Pete thought. He'd remember to say a prayer of thanks later on, but right now, he needed to put some distance between himself and Giovanni Ricci's house. Although he was wearing an empty black backpack on his back, for some reason up until this moment it hadn't occurred to him to put the mask into the backpack. Now, he picked it up from where he'd placed it and did just that. It would be a lot more secure if he was going to be running down the street.

And then the lights in Giovanni Ricci's house came back on.

He was out of breath when he stopped about a block and a half away. He tightened the straps on the backpack, pulled Bob's phone out of his pocket, and held the phone to his mouth.

"Bicycle," he said.

He listened. There was silence on the other end. And then people started talking again. For some reason, he could hear better now; the voices were more distinct.

"What was that?" Giovanni Ricci asked. "Did someone say 'bicycle'"?

"Not someone," Mallory said. "It was my phone."

"Your phone said bicycle?" Ricci asked incredulously.

"Well, it probably wasn't 'bicycle,'" Mallory said. "Just some noise, I think. Something's the matter with my phone. It's happened before. It just makes weird noises from time to time."

"You seem to have trouble with small appliances," Ricci said, a little testily.

"I'm so sorry about the hairdryer," Mallory said. "I'd just never seen one like it before. I plugged it in and turned it on, you know, to sort of test it, and the lights went out. I'm so, so sorry."

Pete grinned. Mallory was so good at coming up with stories. And Giovanni Ricci seemed to be buying this one.

"That's all right," he said to her.

"We should get out of your way now," Mallory said. "We've been too much trouble as it is."

"Yes," Mr. Owusu said. "I'm sorry for the trouble. But after all, this is how interns learn. Thank you again for giving me such an interesting commission."

As Pete listened, Kwame Owusu and Giovanni Ricci said goodbye, and he, Bob, Jupiter, and Mallory left the house and got into Mr. Owusu's truck. In no time at all it had pulled up next to him, where he stood, flashlight in hand, shining it up under his chin.

"Wooooo," he said as spookily as he could.

Only Mallory laughed when he did this. The others were all looking at him intently, and suddenly Pete understood that they wondered where the mask was. Although Mallory had undoubtedly told them the plan once they had gotten back in the truck, only Mallory and Pete had actually seen the mask, and only Mallory really believed he had secured it.

"Don't worry," he said. "It's in my backpack. Let's get out of here."

Pete took the backpack off, cradled it in his arms, and climbed in the back of the truck. Mr. Owusu started driving away, and Mallory asked Pete, "Did you have any trouble?"

"You mean, aside from almost dropping the mask in the nursery and losing Bob's phone in the grass?" Pete asked. "No trouble at all."

"Well done, Second," Jupiter said. "You've come through again."

"But what I want to know," Pete said, "is why it was a good idea to turn all the lights out. It sure made sense when I was going to bust in and create a diversion. But what good did it do just now?"

"I don't know," Mallory said. "You're right. I just thought it would freak Mr. Ricci out and keep him occupied while you climbed in and out of his window."

"But in my house," Pete said, "when there's an outage, my dad starts roaming around checking things out. I was afraid Ricci was going to do that too."

"Luckily he didn't," Bob said. "Mallory told him she'd turned on a hair dryer in the bathroom and that she was afraid he was going to have to call an electrician. I don't think he wanted to leave us alone in his dining room while he went to check and see."

"Anyway," Jupiter said, "I think we left him pretty confused. With any luck, it'll be a while before he realizes the mask is gone. I have to hand it to you, Mallory, and to you, Pete. You showed an excellent ability to modify plans and react to changing circumstances. What a stroke of luck that they actually *were* hiding the mask at Ricci's house, and that you discovered it, Mallory. I can hardly believe you pulled this off. Conning a con artist. You could have quite a life in crime."

"I thought I'd never say this," Mallory said. "But it's all because my mother told me what I thought at the time was a really stupid story about Alyssa Ricci. I'll tell you all about it later. But the greatest thing was the way Mr. Owusu kept talking while Jupiter and I vanished into the Riccis' house. If Mr. Owusu hadn't done that, I don't think this would ever have worked! So thank you, Mr. Owusu!"

"Yes, thank you," Bob said. "For taking us with you, suggesting we wear black, and being so cool and calm!"

They'd gone several blocks when Mr. Owusu said he'd like to stop and take a look at the mask himself. He found a small corner park, with a picnic table under a streetlight, and he pulled the truck over and came to a stop. They all piled out, and Pete carried his backpack over to the table, unbuckled it, and pulled the mask out. The light from the street lamp was thin but good enough to see by, and even though by that time Pete knew the mask pretty well, it still made him feel a little strange.

Mr. Owusu picked up the mask and examined it, as if to see whether he had missed anything important when he had created its reproduction. Pete could see how thrilled Mr. Owusu was to actually be holding the original in his hands. "This is real," he said. "I am certain."

Although he was glad of the confirmation, Pete had already been certain, too. Here on a picnic table in southern California, outside of the stuffy confines of a museum or a private collection or an auction house, was an object Randy Foreman had called the holy grail of African art, and somehow, given what he'd just gone through, Pete could suddenly imagine the days when it had been worn by African tribesmen who had come at night, by torch light and firelight, to administer justice, to restore order, to make things right again.

There were many things about it that Pete could never know, could never understand. He knew that. But he was glad he had played a part in returning the mask to its rightful owner.

The night of the Gala, Califia's mother had told The Three Investigators that Peggy Thomas's husband had been a jazz virtuoso who played tenor sax and piano, and Peggy herself had told them that if she ever got the mask back, she would sell it and use part of the proceeds to set up a foundation which would do what Old Art For Young Artists just pretended to – help deserving young people who weren't as lucky as he, Bob, Jupiter, and Mallory. And now the four of them were on their way to getting that to happen – as a result of an almost perfectly executed plan!

16

A Manichean Mask

Three days later, Bob sat in a butterfly chair in the informal corner of HQ2 making some notes about the case as he waited for Pete, Mallory, and Jupiter — especially Jupiter — to join him. Although he found it awkward to hold his computer in this position, the chair itself was so comfortable he couldn't resist. He hadn't gotten all that far with his notes yet because he kept thinking back over everything that had happened.

The night of the big adventure, after Kwame Owusu had stopped in the pocket park, he had driven the four of them back to the Salvage Yard where they had taken the Fang Ngil mask into HQ1. It was funny, but although it had been Mallory who had first suggested that The Three Investigators had outgrown the mobile home trailer Jupiter's uncle had given them when they were just barely eleven, it had also been Mallory who had said it was the only place in the Salvage Yard safe enough to store the mask.

Uncle Titus and Aunt Mathilda were already in bed by the time the four of them got back, so no one had seen them as they had crunched their way across the gravel to Easy Three – a big oak door, still on its hinges and in its frame, that blocked a clear view of the old trailer, surrounded by piles of salvage. In his arms, Pete had carried the mask – or rather, the black backpack which almost contained it. As Jupiter had opened the lock and led the way down the short passageway to the original side door of the mobile home trailer, it had felt re-assuring to Bob to use the secret entrance.

In fact, when Pete had set the backpack down on the desk in front of the fancy computer Zachary Hughes had given them the year before, there had been an almost audible sigh of relief from all three of them – and Mallory, too. When Jupiter said he thought he'd sleep in HQ1 that night, no one tried to dissuade him. Whether or not the mask was really as valuable as Randy Foreman thought it might be, The Three Investigators felt sure it was the most valuable thing they'd ever had to protect.

While the Medici treasures they'd found in the Napa Valley the summer before had been worth more than the mask – at least if you put them all together – Bob and the others had never been responsible for their safety. But since they'd become responsible for this one ever since they'd decided to steal it, it reassured everyone to think of Jupiter sleeping next to it.

They'd left their camping gear in HQ1, so all Jupiter had to do was to grab his sleeping bag, blow up his air mattress, and lock the door when the three of them headed for their bikes. The next morning, they were all back at the crack of dawn, and as soon as 8:00 rolled around, Bob had called Julian Jackson and told him what had happened.

By 9:00, Julian and Randy were being ushered into HQ2 where Randy examined the mask and confirmed what Kwame Owusu had said – that the Fang Ngil mask was the real deal. By 10:00, they had wedged into his muscle car and were heading for Peggy Thomas's house in Sherman Oaks. No one had called her before they arrived, but she was home, in her studio, dressed in a leotard and tights, and dancing to what she later told them was a recording of her husband, Clay, playing tenor sax.

The six of them stood outside the studio, looking in, and when she had looked up and seen them – Julian holding Pete's backpack aloft – she had instantly known what he held, and by the time she turned off the music and opened the door to let them in, she was crying. Not just crying, but sobbing.

"You got it back?" she said.

"The Three Investigators got it back," Julian said. "Here it is."

As they talked, Bob clearly saw that ever since the six of them had shown up at her house the first time, Peggy had been brooding about how stupid she'd been to give the masks away in the first place – especially without having them properly appraised. She said that even though Clay himself had disliked them and had said they'd given him the willies, as soon as she learned what they'd told her, she'd felt that she'd somehow betrayed his love for her by giving them away so lightly. They weren't his clothes, but they had belonged to him.

She said she knew that was silly, but she just couldn't help it, and that she was so glad to have at least one of them back. By now, several days later, the mask had been delivered to a friend of Cornelius Patterson's, who was an appraiser of African art.

However, the weird thing about the situation at the moment was that, as far as The Three Investigators knew, Giovanni Ricci and his partners had not yet discovered the theft of the real mask and the substitution of the fake one in the Riccis' nursery closet. This was especially weird because, by now, it seemed that half the people in southern California were aware of what had happened.

Not really, of course. But not only had Cornelius Patterson and Lyle Smith been let in on the secret, but when Sabrina Saskatchewan had delivered her daughter Scarlett to Peggy Thomas's dance studio, Peggy Thomas had told *her* what had happened. Sabrina and Scarlett had been so excited by the story that they'd told Scarlett's grandmother, and just the day before, Sibyl Saskatchewan had shown up at the Salvage Yard holding a large shopping bag, and wearing what Bob thought was called a muumuu.

It was turquoise green and festooned with bright red hibiscus flowers. It hung from her shoulders and came to below her knees and looked like a cross between a bathrobe and a shirt. Her hair was again piled on top of her head and fastened with two chopsticks.

Out of the shopping bag, one by one, she'd pulled the four masks they'd worn to the Rocky Beach Summer Theatre Gala.

"Sabrina told me what happened, kiddos," she said. "And I'm sure you remember my promise – that if you caught Old Art red-handed, I'd not only refund the money I was charging you, I'd give you the masks outright, as a memento of the case."

Jupiter said that they hadn't really caught them red-handed *yet*, and that maybe Ms. Saskatchewan might want to wait to hand over the masks until they really did.

"No, no," she said firmly. "Sabrina and Scarlett told me the whole story, and even though you still have some loose ends to tie up, you've done what I wanted you to. There's no way these shady characters can get away with what they're doing much longer. And here's the refund for the rental."

Dumping the contents of her purse on a nearby sofa, she pulled out her wallet, extracted some bills from it, and handed them to Jupiter, who took them politely – and even wrote her a receipt.

Just then, she noticed the wall at the back of HQ2 on which they'd displayed the mementos of their other cases, and, leaving the contents of her purse strewn across the sofa, she went to examine them, with Pete and Mallory's help. Although Bob and Jupiter didn't follow them, Bob could hear from across the room that Pete was saying they'd heard she'd met the Rocky Beach police chief, Chief Reynolds. She laughed gaily. Why, yes, she had, she said — and in circumstances she wouldn't like to repeat!

That was all she said, and soon afterwards, she had gathered her stuff and left. She was a bit of a strange one, but she had kept her word to the letter, Bob thought — and by now, Jupiter and Mallory had already hung the masks she'd given them on the memento wall. They looked great there and would always remind them that this case had started at a masked Venetian ball.

Not only that, but Bob had taken a picture of the masks with his cell phone and shown it to his father the night before — when he'd also given him a blow-by-blow account of everything that had happened since his father's meeting with Larry Winthrop on Sunday night. It had been great to be able to promise him that, if things worked out the way that Jupiter was hoping, Winthrop would never hear from Rémy Gauthier again.

But until The Three Investigators managed to get Old Art For Young Artists to officially close up shop, this case wasn't really over. However, that might happen soon, because by the time Bob saw Jupiter, the First Investigator would have finished a meeting at Peggy Thomas's house in which he, Julian Jackson, and Randy Foreman would have told Giovanni and Alyssa Ricci what The Three Investigators had done.

At first, Jupiter had thought that they should invite the Riccis to HQ2 and try to persuade them that it would be in their best interest to close up Old Art For Young Artists in the manner, and for the reasons, Jupiter had laid out. But when he'd explained the plan to use the Fang Ngil mask as a bargaining chip to Peggy Thomas, she said that since it was her mask, and she'd given The Three Investigators written permission to recover it on her behalf, she wanted to meet the Riccis at her house.

In the end, she'd agreed to let Jupiter, Randy, and Julian attend the meeting. But since she'd thought that having any more people might scare the Riccis off, Pete, Bob, and Mallory had agreed to stay away. Just in case the meeting with the Riccis didn't work, Pete and Mallory were busy using the desk computer and printer in HQ1 to print out everything they could find on the Internet that related to the current situation with Old Art. But just then they came barreling in through the double side doors from the outdoor workshop, carrying folders filled with paper.

"Jupe's here!" Pete said. "We were on our way over when we saw Randy drop him off!"

It took another few minutes, but soon all four of them were sitting in the informal corner of HQ2 – three of them staring at Jupiter intently.

"It worked," Jupiter said. "You were right about Giovanni and Alyssa's marriage, and that Giovanni already wanted to disentangle himself from Old Art. The hardest part of the whole thing was seeing how upset Alyssa Ricci got. Peggy Thomas told her that her husband was in serious trouble, and that she was the only one who could help him. Mrs. Ricci had no idea that her husband had been forging paintings, or that Old Art had been auctioning off the forgeries, then selling the originals to private collectors abroad."

Jupiter shook his head grimly. "She also had no idea that the mask was a valuable piece of African art, or that her husband and his partners had stolen it from the Old Art warehouse.

"The good thing was that Giovanni Ricci didn't try to bluff. He admitted everything at once. And when Peggy Thomas said she'd give them a finder's fee if he'd guarantee that Rémy Gauthier went back to France – either taking his wife with him, or leaving her here – he agreed at once."

"He did?" Pete asked, amazed.

"Yes," Jupiter said. "As I told you when Bob first came up with the idea to use the mask as a bargaining chip, Old Art could probably have made the argument that it owned the mask quite legally, and that it wasn't anyone else's business where they kept it until they sold it at auction. Still, Giovanni Ricci thought Gauthier was smart enough to see the danger of trying that argument on in a court of law. He also thought that whatever Peggy Thomas was willing to give him as a so-called finder's fee would be more than enough to sweeten the deal."

"I still think we could have gotten Gauthier and Guadalupe," Bob said. "And turned them over to the police."

"At least they won't ply their poison in America ever again," Jupiter said. "And that's something."

"So it worked out perfectly!" said Pete. "And if the mask sells for as much as Cornelius's friend thinks it will, she'll have enough left over to stay in her house for the rest of her life, and also set up a *real* foundation. Not to mention setting Jupiter's money worries to rest! At least if Peggy Thomas keeps her word about *our* finder's fee!"

"She will," Jupiter said. "After Giovanni and Alyssa left, she mentioned it again. She also wants to give Julian and Randy money for graduate school. As for us, this has proved to be a much more significant case than we could have imagined when it started."

Jupiter went to the desk in the office section of HQ2 and pulled out five black document clips from the top drawer, like paper clips, but fancier. Bob knew what came next.

"Two years ago," Jupiter said, "when we had a different windfall on our hands, I suggested we divide it into five equal parts." He put the document clips on the desktop. "Three parts went to our individual college funds, and two parts went into a firm account." He separated the clips out – three and two. "At the time, Mallory wasn't with the firm, so we didn't include her in our thinking."

"Oh, yes, you did," Mallory said. "You commissioned my immigrant's chest. The day you took me to Leif and Magnus's workshop, and I saw it for the first time, I knew I wanted to stay in California."

"That was the day you gave us the advertising poster," Bob said, gesturing to the frame on the memento wall that featured the words CALIFORNIA, CORNUCOPIA OF THE WORLD."

"Anyway," Mallory said, "the point I'm making is that I couldn't have cared less that you didn't set a document clip aside for me."

"I'm sure that's true," Jupiter said. "Nonetheless, *this* time I want you to get one for your college fund. And I want *all* of our college funds to be equal. In other words, I want to make up now for what we didn't do two years ago. If Pete and Bob agree, at least."

"Of course!" Bob said.

Pete grinned. "So we'll put whatever's left over in the Three Investigators' firm account?"

"Yes," Jupiter said, separating the document clips on the desktop. Pete leapt to his feet, picked one of them up and pushed it around the desk, making vroom-vroom-vroom sounds – just as he had the first time.

"And maybe we can use some of it to get a muscle car like Randy's!" he said.

"Ixnay," Jupiter said. "No doughnuts and no muscle cars. But I think we'll be able to stop worrying about whether we spent too much money on HQ2. We were very lucky in the way this all played out."

"We really were," Mallory said. "But so were Giovanni and Alyssa Ricci. I'm glad they'll be able to have their baby without Alyssa worrying that her husband might get arrested and taken off to jail! The more cases we investigate, the more I see what a blunt instrument the law really is."

Jupiter swept the document clips back into their drawer. Then he and Pete rejoined Mallory and Bob in the corner with the butterfly chairs.

As Pete settled down, he said, "O.K. Now comes the fun part. It's called 'What Will Bob Name This One?' It has to be The Mystery of the Something Mask. I just don't know what the something is." He paused dramatically. "Though I remember Bob telling us his father said that if he was fired, at least he'd have more time to write the stuff he wants to write, instead of puff pieces about Machiavellian villains. I bet nobody thought I was listening, but I was."

Mallory and Jupiter both laughed. Bob had also been thinking about his father's comment. "I agree with Jupiter that a bunch of the criminals we've run into aren't just deceitful, but also manipulative and callous. But in a way that's the problem. 'Machiavellian' isn't specific enough to describe what Old Art was doing."

"That's right," Mallory said. "Using reverse racism as a cover for forgery and theft was diabolically clever. People like Kwame Owusu bring their families to America because they expect they'll be treated respectfully and be able to prosper here. Nobody gave Kwame Owusu an immigrant's chest, but America *did* give him the opportunity to make a life for himself. Pitting people of different races against one another is vile − and it's not what this country is about."

"Actually, my father just taught me another M word, too," Bob said. "He told me that Manicheanism was an ancient Persian religion that saw life in dualistic terms, and that in a lot of schools in the United States, kids are being taught that the world is a never-ending battle for power between oppressors and the people they're oppressing."

"*The Mystery of the Manichean Mask!*" Pete said. "But what would the mask part of it mean?"

"I don't know," Bob said honestly. "Even though you could say that Old Art For

Young Artists was set up as a Manichean enterprise, I'm not sure how you could call that a 'mask'."

Jupiter had been silent ever since he'd swept the document clips back into the desk drawer, but now he turned to Bob.

"You said that when you and Mallory were eavesdropping at the Gala, you thought that the 'mask' Rémy Gauthier and Juanita Guadalupe were talking about was metaphorical."

"That's right," Bob said. "Mallory thought that maybe they were talking about camouflaging something."

"Well, even though it turned out to be an actual mask, why not think of the title as having that other meaning, instead? *Manichean Mask* would refer to the way in which human beings like to conceal the complexity of existence behind a kind of camouflage – a camouflage pretending that everything is simple," Jupiter suggested. "Good and bad, dark and light. Us and them."

"That's a great idea," Bob said. "Like the people who got in touch with Larry Winthrop to try to get my father fired. To them, life is a fight between two groups of people, with *us* the good guys and *them* the enemy who has to be destroyed!"

"I like it," Pete said suddenly. "And what's even better, I get it!"

"It's an excellent title," Mallory agreed. "But in spite of everything good that's come out of this case, I still sort of wish it had never happened in the first place."

"I know what you mean," Pete said. "I couldn't believe it when Juanita Guadalupe offered me an internship and then turned Jupiter down! Everyone knows you can't judge a book by its cover, but those Old Art con men certainly did!"

Pete was right about that, Bob thought. The reason Old Art had gotten away with what it was doing was that a lot of people were so scared of being called a racist these days that they'd far rather actually *be* one.

People were perfectly happy to glance in your direction, and, without even speaking with you, arrive at a whole bunch of conclusions about who you were — most of them probably flat out wrong. Bob wanted to see himself, and be seen by other people, as Bob Andrews, and nothing else. He knew his friends saw him that way, but he remembered how he'd felt when Juanita Guadalupe had seen him as just another Asian.

He also remembered how restful it had felt at the Gala when he had worn the bobcat mask. No one could see his face and make assumptions about who he was; ever since he could remember, he'd felt wretched when people had made assumptions about him on the basis of how he looked.

He was just about to share this thought with the others when he stopped himself. After all, there was nothing unusual about feeling that way. In fact, he imagined that just about anyone who had ever been born had felt, at some point or other, that the way they looked on the outside didn't match the way they felt on the inside. Everyone was constantly being seen as somebody they just plain weren't.

He thought Mallory probably had to deal with this all the time – because of her red hair and because she wasn't a typical girl. And Jupiter – at least in the days when people called him "stocky" – probably him too. And if anyone thought of Pete as just another dumb jock, they were in for a big surprise. And what about Randy Foreman? He might look like a California surfer driving a muscle car, but he was studying the history of the early 20th century avant-garde in Paris.

But that was just the way of the world,

Bob thought. And since there would never be a world in which everyone withheld judgment until they got to know you, the important thing was for *you* to know who you were — not who someone else thought you were, or who you wished you were or wanted to be, but who you honestly truly were, with all your strengths and weaknesses and foibles, all your likable and dislikable qualities. And to have friends who knew who you were, too.

As for what Mallory had said about wishing this case had never happened in the first place, although Pete might agree with her, Bob didn't. For one thing, Bob had liked meeting Kwame Owusu. For another, he knew it would please his father to have had their conversation about Manicheanism inspire the title for the case. And for a third, he felt proud of having come up with the negotiating strategy that Jupiter had used successfully, in the end.

Although he hadn't mentioned it when he got back from Peggy Thomas's house, when Bob had first suggested that they use the mask as a bargaining chip to put Old Art For Young Artists out of business, Jupiter had said that if the idea worked out, he'd be giving Bob full credit for it — and Bob was sure that in his heart, he did.

And besides all that, Bob was glad the case had happened because if it hadn't, he and Pete might never have had that talk about Califia and *West Side Story*, and Pete would never have said it was great to have a girl-friend, or asked him if he'd thought about dating Freya Haldorsson.

Although he'd told Pete he'd have to think about it, at this point he'd done that, and decided it was an excellent idea. He'd been comfortable with Freya from the start – if a little nonplussed to find himself the object of a girl's ardent crush. And such a pretty girl! With her wide eyes and glowing skin and winning smile, she was lovely.

That afternoon when he was back at work in the library, shelving books again, he kept thinking about the case, and as he started to shove the popular horror novel *Hiding In Plain Sight* back into place on the shelves for the second time in a week, he paused to look again at its dust jacket.

As before, he observed that the artist had depicted a malevolent figure hiding behind a painted wooden screen – a screen on which a group of children were having a picnic by a river that sparkled in the sun – and, as before, he thought that since you really *couldn't* judge a book by its cover, whatever this particular book might be about, it was almost certainly not that.

Even so, the artist was onto something, Bob reflected, as he finished putting the book on the shelf. Behind an eye-catching screen of shining light and shadowed darkness – a screen in which black and white, good and evil, were easy to tell apart – lay the complex place in which human beings really lived. Not only did almost all people have both good and bad qualities, but an awful lot of them were almost irresistibly drawn to the idea that certain types of people were good and other types were bad – and not just in novels, but in real life.

The trouble was, although horror stories – and also certain types of mysteries – gave people the reassurance that wicked actors would always be seen for what they were, life itself wasn't like that. In life, people pretending to be virtuous or victimized or oppressed were frequently just the opposite. In life, the evil often masqueraded as the good, and got away with it.

That, Bob thought, was the secret always hiding in plain sight.

ABOUT THE AUTHORS

Elizabeth Arthur

Elizabeth was born on November 15, 1953 in New York City. She is the daughter of Robert Arthur, the creator of The Three Investigators series. She was educated at Concord Academy in Concord, Massachusetts, the University of Michigan in Ann Arbor, Michigan, Notre Dame University of Nelson, British Columbia, and the University of Victoria in Victoria, British Columbia.

Before she started working on the New Three Investigators series in December of 2018, Elizabeth spent most of her life writing for adults. *Island Sojourn* – a memoir about building a house on a wilderness island in northern Canada – was published in 1980 by Harper and Row. A second memoir, *Looking For The Klondike Stone*, was published by Knopf in 1992. She is also the author of the novels *Beyond the Mountain, Bad Guys, Binding Spell, Antarctic Navigation,* and *Bring Deeps*.

Elizabeth's writing has received fellowships, grants, and awards from the Bread Loaf Writer's Conference, the Ossabaw Island Project, the Vermont Council on the Arts, and the

Indiana Arts Commission. She twice received fellowships from the National Endowment for the Arts and was the first novelist ever given an Antarctic Artists and Writers Operational Support Grant from the National Science Foundation.

Her novel *Antarctic Navigation* was chosen by the New York *Times* as a Notable Book, received a Critics' Choice Award from the San Francisco *Review of Books*, and was chosen as a Best Book of 1995 by *A Common Reader*. In 1996 the novel received the Ohioana Book Award for Fiction from the Ohioana Library Association.

Elizabeth has also taught creative writing at Miami University in Oxford, Ohio; the University of Cincinnati; and Indiana University/Purdue University of Indianapolis, where she directed the creative writing program. She and Steven Bauer met in 1980 at the Bread Loaf Writer's Conference and have been married since June of 1982.

Steven Bauer

Steven was born on September 10, 1948 in Newark, New Jersey. He was educated at Hanover Park High School in East Hanover, New Jersey, Trinity College in Hartford, Connecticut, and the University of Massachusetts in Amherst, Massachusetts. In 1970 he received a B.A. with Honors in English from Trinity, and in 1975 he received an M.F.A. in English from the University of Massachusetts.

Steven is the author of three books for young people – *Satyrday*, 1980; *The Strange and Wonderful Tale of Robert McDoodle*, 1999; and *A Cat of a Different Color*, 2000. His book of poems *Daylight Savings* was published by Gibbs Smith in 1989 and won the Peregrine Smith Poetry Prize.

Steven's work has received fellowships from the Bread Loaf Writer's Conference and the Fine Arts Work Center in Provincetown, Massachusetts. In addition, he has been given grants and awards from the American Library Association, the Parents' Choice Foundation, the Ossabaw Island Project, the Massachusetts Arts Council, and the Indiana Arts Commission.

From 1979 to 1982, Steven taught literature and creative writing at Colby College in Waterville, Maine. From 1982 to 2009 he taught at Miami University in Oxford, Ohio where he directed the graduate and undergraduate creative writing programs. In 2010 he established Hollow Tree Literary Services, an independent editing business.